I0545698

PIT PERFECT MURDER

A BARKSIDE OF THE MOON COZY MYSTERY
BOOK ONE

RENEE GEORGE

BARKSIDE OF THE MOON PRESS

Pit Bulls are Sweet . . .and that's no mystery!

When cougar-shifter Lily Mason moves to Moonrise, Missouri, she wishes for only three things from the town and its human population. . . to find a job, to find a place to live, and to live as a human, not a therianthrope.

Lily gets more than she bargains for when a rescue pit bull named Smooshie rescues her from an oncoming car, and it's love at first sight. Thanks to Smooshie, Lily's first two wishes are granted by Parker Knowles, the owner of the Pit Bull Rescue center, who offers her a job at the shelter and the room over his garage for rent.

Lily's new life as an integrator is threatened when Smooshie finds Katherine Kapersky, the local church choir leader and head of the town council, dead in the field behind the rescue center. Unfortunately, there are more suspects than mourners for the elderly town leader. Can Lily keep her less-than-human status under wraps? Or will the killer, who has pulled off a nearly Pit Perfect murder, expose her to keep Lily and her dog from digging up the truth?

For Kona, my lovable pittie partner in crime.
You have filled my heart and because of you
I am aware.

I have to thank two ladies who help me tremendously with my books. BFF Michele Bardsley, the best critique partner around. She really helps me turn lumps of coal into zirconias. And my BFF sister, Robbin, who never holds back on giving a reader's point of view. She lets me get away with NOTHING. She says, you're welcome. Then follows the usual suspects, BFF Dakota Cassidy, who spends several weeknights on the phone with me as we talk each other down. There is no one else I'd want to be out on that ledge with, darling! And a big thank you to my awesome editor Kelli Collins, who keeps me straight!

I also have to thank my Rebels. You guys offer me so much love and support. You keep me motivated! Even on my lowest days, you all raise me up. I'm so lucky to have such a great group of readers surrounding me everyday!

I want to thank Missouri Pit Bull Rescue located in Kansas City Missouri (http://www.mopitbullrescue.org/). Their website gave me so much information about what it takes to rescue these beautiful, loving animals, I would encourage you to peruse their website, adopt if you are up for the commitment, foster if you can only help short term, or donate your time or money to help this shelter grow and rescue even more pit bulls in crisis.

And lastly, I'd like to thank that dark, hot witches brew known as black coffee for keeping me going. Without you, I'd get nothing done. Like ever.

When I was eighteen years old, I came home from a sleepover and found my mom and dad with their throats cut, and their hearts ripped from their chests.

My little brother Danny was in a broom closet in the kitchen, his arms wrapped around his knees, and his face pale and ghostly. Until that day, I'd planned to go to college and study medicine after graduation, but instead, I ended up staying home and taking care of my seven-year-old brother.

Seventeen years later, my brother was murdered. At the time, Danny's death looked like it would go unsolved, much like my parents' had.

Without Haze Kinsey, my best friend since we were five, the killers would have gotten away with it. She was a special agent for the FBI for almost a decade, and when I called her about Danny's death, she dropped everything to come help me get him justice. The evil group of witches and Shifters responsible for the decimation of my family paid with their lives.

Yes. I said witches and Shifters. Did I forget to mention I'm a werecougar? Oh, and my friend Hazel is a witch. Recently, I discovered witches in my own family tree on my mother's side. Shifters, in general, only mated with Shifters, but witches were the exception. As a matter of fact, my friend Haze is mated to a bear Shifter.

I wouldn't have known about the witch in my genealogy, though, if a rogue witch coven hadn't done some funky hoodoo witchery to me. Apparently, the spell activated a latent talent that had been dormant in my hybrid genes.

My ancestor's magic acted like truth serum to anyone who came near her. No one could lie in her presence. Lucky me, my ability was a much lesser form of hers. People didn't have to tell me the truth, but whenever they were around me, they had the compulsion to over-share all sorts of private matters about themselves. This can get seriously uncomfortable for all parties involved. Like, the fact that I didn't need to know that Janet Strickland had been wearing the same pair of underwear for an entire week, or that Mike Dandridge had sexual fantasies about clowns.

My newfound talent made me unpopular and unwelcome in a town full of paranormal creatures who thrived on little deceptions. So, when Haze discovered the whereabouts of my dad's brother, a guy I hadn't known even existed, I sold all my belongings, let the bank have my parents' house, jumped in my truck, and headed south.

After two days and 700 miles of nonstop gray, snowy weather, I pulled my screeching green and yellow mini-truck into an auto repair shop called The Rusty Wrench. Much like my beloved pickup, I'd needed a new start, and moving to a small town occupied by humans seemed the best shot. I'd barely made it to Moonrise, Missouri before my truck began its death throes. The vehicle protested the last 127 miles by sputtering to a halt as I rolled her into the closest spot.

The shop was a small white-brick building with a one-car garage off to the right side. A black SUV and a white compact car occupied two of the six parking spots.

A sign on the office door said: *No Credit Cards. Cash Only. Some Local Checks Accepted (Except from Earl—You Know Why, Earl! You check-bouncing bastard).*

A man in stained coveralls, wiping a greasy tool with a rag, came out the side door of the garage. He had a full head of wavy gray hair, bushy eyebrows over light blue, almost colorless eyes, and a minimally lined face that made me wonder about his age. I got out of the truck to greet him.

"Can I help you, miss?" His voice was soft and raspy with a strong accent that was not quite Deep South.

"Yes, please." I adjusted my puffy winter coat. "The

heater stopped working first. Then the truck started jerking for the last fifty miles or so."

He scratched his stubbly chin. "You could have thrown a rod, sheared the distributor, or you have a bad ignition module. That's pretty common on these trucks."

I blinked at him. I could name every muscle in the human body and twelve different kinds of viruses, but I didn't know a spark plug from a radiator cap. "And that all means…"

"If you threw a rod, the engine is toast. You'll need a new vehicle."

"Crap." I grimaced. "What if it's the other thingies?"

The scruffy mechanic shrugged. "A sheared distributor is an easy fix, but I have to order in the part, which means it won't get fixed for a couple of days. Best-case scenario, it's the ignition module. I have a few on hand. Could get you going in a couple of hours, but…" he looked over my shoulder at the truck and shook his head, "…I wouldn't get your hopes up."

I must've looked really forlorn because the guy said, "It might not need any parts. Let me take a look at it first. You can grab a cup of coffee across the street at Langdon's One-Stop."

He pointed to the gas station across the road. It didn't look like much. The pale-blue paint on the front of the building looked in need of a new coat, and the weather-beaten sign with the store's name on it had seen better days. There was a car at the gas pumps and a couple more in the parking lot, but not enough to call it busy.

I'd had enough of one-stops, though, thank you. The bathrooms had been horrible enough to make a wereraccoon yark, and it took a lot to make those garbage eaters sick. Besides, I wasn't just passing through Moonrise, Missouri.

"Have you ever heard of The Cat's Meow Café?" Saying the name out loud made me smile the way it had when Hazel had first said it to me. I'd followed my GPS into town, so I knew I wasn't too far away from the place.

"Just up the street about two blocks, take a right on Sterling Street. You can't miss it. I should have some news in about an hour or so, but take your time."

"Thank you, Mister…"

"Greer." He shoved the tool in his pocket. "Greer Knowles."

"I'm Lily Mason."

"Nice to meet ya," said Greer. "The place gets hoppin' around noon. That's when church lets out."

I looked at my phone. It was a little before noon now. "Good. I could go for something to eat. How are the burgers?"

"Best in town," he quipped.

I laughed. "Good enough."

Even in the sub-freezing temperature, my hands were sweating in my mittens. I wasn't sure what had me more nervous, leaving the town I grew up in for the first time in my life or meeting an uncle I'd never known existed.

I crossed a four-way intersection. One of the signs was missing, and I saw the four-by-four post had snapped off at its base. I hadn't noticed it on my way in. Crap. Had I run a stop sign? I walked the two blocks to Sterling. The diner was just where Greer had said. A blue truck, a green mini-coup, and a sheriff's SUV were parked out front.

An alarm dinged as the glass door opened to The Cat's Meow. Inside, there was a row of six booths along the wall, four tables that seated four out in the open floor, and counter seating with about eight cushioned black stools. The interior décor was rustic country with orange tabby kitsch everywhere. A man in blue jeans and a button-down shirt with a string tie sat in the nearest booth. A female police officer sat at a counter chair sipping coffee and eating a cinnamon roll. Two elderly women, one with snowball-white hair, the other a dyed strawberry-blonde, sat in a back booth.

The white poof-headed lady said, "This egg is not over-medium."

"Well, call the mayor," said Redhead. "You're unhappy with your eggs. Again."

"See this?" She pointed at the offending egg. "Slime, right here. Egg snot. You want to eat it?"

"If it'll make you shut up about breakfast food, I'll eat it and lick the plate."

A man with copper-colored hair and a thick beard, tall and well-muscled, stepped out of the kitchen. He wore a white apron around his waist, and he had on a black T-shirt and blue jeans. He held a plate with a single fried egg shining in the middle.

The old woman with the snowy hair blushed, her thin skin pinking up as he crossed the room to their table. "Here you go, Opal. Sorry 'bout the mix-up on your egg." He slid the plate in front of her. "This one is pure perfection." He grinned, his broad smile shining. "Just like you." He winked.

Opal giggled.

The redhead rolled her eyes. "You're as easy as the eggs."

"Oh, Pearl. You're just mad he didn't flirt with you."

As the women bickered over the definition of flirting, the cook glanced at me. He seemed startled to see me there. "You can sit anywhere," he said. "Just pick an open spot."

"I'm actually looking for someone," I told him.

"Who?"

"Daniel Mason." Saying his name gave me a hollow ache. My parents had named my brother Daniel, which told me my dad had loved his brother, even if he didn't speak about him.

The man's brows rose. "And why are you looking for him?"

I immediately knew he was a werecougar like me. The scent was the first clue, and his eyes glowing, just for a second, was another. "You're Daniel Mason, aren't you?"

He moved in closer to me and whispered barely audibly, but with my Shifter senses, I heard him loud and clear. "I go by Buzz these days."

"Who's your new friend, Buzz?" the policewoman asked. Now that she was looking up from her newspaper, I could see she was young.

He flashed a charming smile her way. "Never you mind, Nadine." He gestured to a waitress, a middle-aged woman with sandy-colored hair, wearing a black T-shirt and a blue jean skirt. "Top off her coffee, Freda. Get Nadine's mind on something other than me."

"That'll be a tough 'un, Buzz." Freda laughed. "I don't think Deputy Booth comes here for the cooking."

"More like the cook," the elderly lady with the light strawberry-blonde hair said. She and her friend cackled.

The policewoman's cheeks turned a shade of crimson

that flattered her chestnut-brown hair and pale complexion. "Y'all mind your P's and Q's."

Buzz chuckled and shook his head. He turned his attention back to me. "Why is a pretty young thing like you interested in plain ol' me?"

I detected a slight apprehension in his voice.

"If you're Buzz Mason, I'm Lily Mason, and you're my uncle."

The man narrowed his dark-emerald gaze at me. "I think we'd better talk in private."

CHAPTER 2

Buzz's office was a small room at the back of the kitchen. He gestured for me to sit in a wooden chair in front of his desk then crossed his arms and leaned back against the wall. "What are you doing here, Lily?"

"So you know who I am?"

"If Jack sent you after me, you can tell him I'm not coming home. How'd he even find me?"

"My dad is dead." I instantly regretted being so blunt. Buzz dropped his arms to his sides, his face ashen with shock. "I'm sorry," I said. "It's been so long for me now, I didn't think."

"How long?"

"Seventeen years ago."

"And Constance? How is she holding up?"

I shook my head. "She's dead too."

He moved behind his desk and sat down, his hands shaking as he scratched his beard. "The last time I heard from Jack, you'd just been born. I told him I never wanted to hear from him again." His voice was choked with grief. He looked up at me. His liquid gaze held me. "How?"

"They were murdered. Some stupid druid ritual."

"Druids? They don't usually mix with our kind."

"It was actually a witch and some Shifters who were practicing druidic magic. Their power fed on the pain of their victims."

Buzz's face reddened, and I could smell a faint whiff of acrid anger. "Christ Almighty."

"You really have integrated," I observed. In the para-normal world, most followed the teachings of the Goddess. It was rare to find a Christian amongst Shifters or witches, so to hear my uncle invoke the name of the Christian God's son fascinated me.

"How did you find me?"

"My best friend used to work for the FBI."

"Another integrator?"

"Sort of. Hazel is a witch, but she lived and worked with humans before moving back to Paradise Falls."

"Land sakes, I never thought I'd hear that name again."

His eyes softened with nostalgia, and for a painful second, he reminded me of my dad.

"Sooo, do I call you Uncle Buzz?"

"Uh, no." He held up his hands. "I might be forty years older than you, but these humans will see us as much closer in age. We'll say we're cousins."

"I've never really hung around with humans."

"Then this ought to be a real treat." He rubbed his hand over his hair. "For as long as it lasts. You can't stay, Lily."

"You've managed to hide from these people. If you can do it, so can I."

"I've had forty years of experience fooling humans, girl. I made a lot of mistakes in the beginning. I've only been in Moonrise for a handful of years, and if things go well, I can stay here for another fifteen or twenty before folks start wondering why I'm not looking a lot older."

The soft dip at the apex of his upper lip revealed long-standing grief.

"You look a lot like him," I said.

"Who?"

"My dad."

"Fine." Buzz sighed. "You can stay for a little while, but I have a one-bedroom trailer and no place to keep you."

"I'll find a place to stay." Surely they had a B&B or a local motel. I didn't have much money, but it would be enough to get me by for a few weeks.

"Buzz," Freda yelled back. "You got customers. Church crowd's coming in."

"Busiest time of the week," Buzz said. He ushered me out of the chair and toward the door. "Go get some lunch." With a wink, he added, "On me."

I sat on one of the counter stools. The vinyl covering was a bit rough on its pipe-seam edges and snagged on my chocolate-brown leggings. Luckily, it didn't tear a hole. I placed my coat on the seat next to me.

"Hey, there. I'm Freda." The waitress stood across the counter from me and pointed to her name tag. "Can I get you started with some coffee?"

"Yes, please." The heat in the diner made me realize just how cold I'd been. "That would be great."

She slid a laminated menu across to me. "Be right up, sugar."

"No sugar," I said.

She looked at me funny.

"I like my coffee just straight black."

"Oh." She smiled. "I got ya." She winked. "I'll leave off bringing the cream and sugar around."

"Thanks, Freda. I'm Lily, by the way."

She smiled again. "Nice to meet you, Lily."

A few moments later, she came back with a piping-hot cup of black coffee.

"You know what you want to eat yet?"

"I'll take the triple-decker bacon burger with double cheese, double bacon. All the fixings and a side of fries."

Freda raised a brow, her lip curling on one side into an amused smirk. "Where you going to put all that food, honey? You're just a tiny little thang."

"I have hollow legs," I said seriously.

"Just like your cousin. He's a helluva good cook, and the way he eats, it's no wonder." She laughed. It was a nice sound. "Buzz," she hollered as she traversed to the kitchen window and hung the check. "Order in."

The coffee was good and hot. Freshly brewed. I liked that the diner didn't let a pot sit around all day after breakfast. Fifteen minutes later, my food arrived. The three beef patties were thick and juicy, four slices of bacon, and lots of gooey cheese made my mouth water. I inhaled the delicious fire-grilled aroma. On the side, there was a large tomato slice, onions, and hamburger pickle chips. The bun was buttered and toasted to perfection. And the fries... Oh my goodness, the fries. They were thick cut, crispy on the outside... I took a bite. Tender on the inside. Salted just right. Sheer nirvana.

"Are you okay?" Freda asked. "You look like you're having a religious experience."

I giggled as I ate another fry. "I think I am." Uncle Buzz made an awesome burger. I took another big bite and resisted the urge to hum.

The booths had filled up with families in a wide variety of ages and dressed in their finest clothes. A woman with hair the color of margarine walked in and dusted her feet on the welcome mat. She wore an expensive wool and cashmere double-breasted coat. The collar was high on her neck, and the hem hit her mid-thigh. The narrow shoulders fit her slim figure and made her appear classically regal. By the way she scanned the room, I was certain it was the appearance she wanted to affect.

I'd seen her kind before and suffered the slings and arrows of their sharp tongues. I hunched my shoulders and then forced myself to relax. I had nothing to fear from a human.

She cast a gaze at the man sitting nearest the door, the one who wore the string tie.

"I didn't see you in church this morning, Edward."

He barely looked up from his coffee. "It's not against the law, Katie. Otherwise, you'd have sent the sheriff."

She hushed her voice, but with my cougar ears, I could easily hear her words. "How does is look to have my own brother miss Rex's service?"

Edward didn't bother trying to match her lower tone. "*You* married a preacher. Not me." Several of the patrons shifted uncomfortably as the mood of the diner sobered.

"He's a reverend, Edward. Not a two-bit preacher."

"I'm sure God could care less about titles."

The woman he called Katie stood up straight and looked as if she would say more, but a man walked in behind her. "Let's get a seat, Katherine," he said. He looked at the man seated in the booth. "Afternoon, Ed."

Edward nodded. "Rex."

Ah, the reverend husband. It felt odd listening in on their conversation from across the room, but I grew up in a town where privacy only happened at home and sometimes not even then. There are no secret conversations in a room full of Shifters.

"Heya, Reverend Kapersky. Mrs. Kapersky," Freda said to the couple with less enthusiasm than when she'd greeted me. "Y'all have a seat, and I'll come 'round with some coffee."

Whispers began as they sat at the last open table. "I hate

her," I heard someone say. "Shhh," said another. "Old bat is going to take it too far one day."

My uncle came out of the back. "Afternoon, Rev." He smirked and winked at Katherine Kapersky. "Aren't you looking like a ripe peach on a hot summer day?"

"Uh-huh," she replied. "The next council meeting, you won't be such a wise-cracker."

"You know you don't want a food chain coming in and killing local business."

"Well, you ain't exactly local, are you, Buzz?"

The cop Nadine slid from her seat just a few places down from me. "Buzz has been here long enough for us to count him as hometown, Mrs. Kapersky."

Freda positioned herself between Buzz and the vile woman. "That's the truth," she added.

Katherine eyed the waitress and the young female officer with disdain. "You shut it, Nadine Booth. If you ever want to be sheriff, you'll keep in mind who you disrespect."

"Like you'd ever throw your hat in for me," Nadine mumbled.

"Let it go," my uncle said. He smiled again at the unlikeable woman. "The usual for y'all? Wedge salad for the missus and a BLT for you, Rev?"

In reply, Katherine Kapersky took off her jacket and handed it to Freda to hang up before she sat down.

"Thank you, Buzz. That'd be nice," Reverend Kapersky said.

I wished I could say I'd never met anyone as miserable as the Kapersky woman, but unfortunately, people like her were always around.

Freda took a tray with a BLT on toasted sourdough, and a wedge of lettuce with bacon crumbles, finely diced tomatoes, chopped chives, crisply tart Granny Smith apple slices, and finished off with a creamy bleu cheese dressing (according to the menu) to the reverend and his sourpuss wife.

"Enjoy," Freda said, and somehow managed to make the nicety imply that they could, "choke on it." Katherine Kapersky didn't even acknowledge Freda. I hated to pass judgment on someone I didn't know, but this Katie woman made it easy. She was terrible with a heaping side of bitter.

"Ow!" she shouted and spit a mouthful of salad onto her plate. She picked up a small piece of bacon, examined it and put it back down, her expression sour.

"Are you all right, dear?" Reverend Rex asked benignly.

Buzz came out of the kitchen. "What happened?"

She glared at him. "Other than your bacon being hard

as a rock, everything is just peachy." To her husband, she said, "I think I chipped a crown."

"I'm sorry, Katie. You want something else from the kitchen? I have cherry pie." He smiled.

I saw the woman soften for a microsecond before her expression once again matched her unpleasant personality. "So I can choke on a pit? No, thank you."

I heard someone mutter how they'd like to choke *her*.

Katherine Kapersky pushed her plate aside and hissed to her husband, "Hurry up."

With great tolerance, the reverend pushed his plate forward and stood up to get his coat on.

Buzz shook his head but held his tongue. "Have a nice day, folks." He wiggled his brows as he passed me on the way back to the kitchen. "Welcome to Moonrise, Lily."

CHAPTER 3

An hour later, I waited at the intersection by the garage, the one with the broken sign. Traffic was light, but I still had to wait for a few cars and trucks. A young man in a full-size gray pickup gestured to me to cross. I gave him a wave of thanks and headed to the other side.

A blaring horn startled me. "Look out!" I heard someone shout.

Behind me, a black sedan zoomed past the broken sign and raced toward me.

My first impulse was to use my cougar strength to leap away from harm, but something slammed into me from behind, and I landed several feet from the street. I rolled to my back and blinked up at the heavy beast that had just saved my life.

A dog. A great big dog, white and rusty-brown in color,

stood over me with its tongue lolling to one side as its ears twitched left and right. Its wide mouth split its adorable face in a smile. Its breath was something to behold—somewhere between sweaty socks and spoiled lima beans. Poor baby needed a mint!

I sat up. It sniffed at me. I sniffed back. I could tell by the lack of über-charged testosterone in the dog's scent *she* was female.

"Good girl," I said, running my hand over her chest and front quarter. She thanked me by licking the side of my face.

I laughed.

All this sounds like it took minutes, but really it was seconds. A man grabbed the dog by the collar and pulled her back as I got up from the asphalt.

"Are you okay?" the guy asked.

"I'm fine." And for the first time since I'd left Paradise Falls, I really felt okay. I stood up, dusting the snow and street from my puffy winter coat as we got out of the road. I noticed with more than a little disgust that my leggings had a hole in the right knee. Still, it was better than being road kill. "Your dog saved me." I smiled at the pittie and scratched under her chin. "She's a real beauty."

"Hold up, girl." He gently tugged the dog. "Wow, I've never seen her this excited."

"She's a hero," I told him. I took off my gloves and knelt down to rub her cheeks, enjoying the warmth on my hands. "Aren't you?" I devolved into baby talk. "Yes, you are. Such a good-good girl. A sweet baby. Yes, you are."

The dog yanked free of the dude and leaned her body into mine, her wiggly butt gyrating as her giant tail whacked me. The only other time I remember getting tail-whacked like that was when my brother and I played together in our cougar forms. He used to think it was hilarious to tail-smack me. The bittersweet memory made me sigh.

The dog, as if sensing my melancholy, wedged herself under my arm as if she were trying to hug me. I can't explain what happened next because I'd never felt anything like it before. A wave of utter adoration washed over me.

I fell in love with this furry bundle of energy.

"She really likes you." He said it as if she didn't like everyone. A baby as sweet as she was, I found it hard to believe she wasn't the most popular pet in town.

"Aww, come here," I said, looping my arms around her and scratching down her back. I let my gaze go to the man who'd tried to rescue me from my rescuer—and froze.

He was tall and broadly built, though it was hard to tell

how much was him and how much was his winter coat. He had dark-brown hair and ocean-blue eyes. I caught the scent of honey and mint on him. Most likely a cologne or body spray. It smelled really nice.

His square jaw worked back and forth as he considered me. "Are you new in town?"

"I'm not from here, if that's what you mean." The dog licked my hands. I brushed my palms over her ears. "Aren't you so smooshie? Such a sweet smooshie girl. What's her name?"

He smiled, and my stomach dipped. "Smooshie sounds like a great name."

"Doesn't she already have a name?"

"I've been calling her 'girl' mostly."

I noticed then the scars around the dog's cheeks, but she looked healthy otherwise.

As if he could read my mind, he said, "I own a pit bull rescue. She was in a foster home for a couple of months with some friends of mine, but they just couldn't take care of her anymore, and we've been having trouble finding someone to adopt her." He crossed his arms. "You wouldn't be interested in adopting Smooshie, would you?"

My stomach squeezed, and my chest filled with heartache for the dog. I knew him saying the dog's name, calling her Smooshie, was a ploy to play on my sympathy, but this sweet girl had me at first lick.

"I think she's adopted me," I finally said. "So I guess I have to let her take care of me." Smooshie licked my hand, her long tongue getting into every crevice between my fingers. I'm sure the hamburger I'd scarfed played a huge role in her attentive kisses.

"Good." He clicked a leash onto her collar. "I think you two are a perfect fit. You really seem to know your way around a dog. You ever own one?"

"No," I said. But I am a Shifter, I didn't believe in owning animals. Despite the whole cat-versus-dog stereotypes, werecats, in general, didn't mind were-wolves. Or dogs. Especially this one. "We'll be friends," I told Smooshie. The dog wiggled happily.

The man's blue eyes sparkled as his gaze met mine. "I'm Parker, by the way."

I had a moment of clarity meeting Smooshie and Parker. It reminded me of the time when I was five years old, and I was forced (and I mean physically) to attend Paradise Falls Elementary School. My mother and father had walked me to PFE on a mild August morning, kissed me on the forehead (after ten minutes of prying my claws—yes, I'd partially shifted into my Were form—from their legs), and ushered me to the long line of students waiting outside the front doors.

I'd always been a solitary soul. I'd easily entertained myself for hours during the day, which made me a great child for my parents, but scored me zero points on the social interaction scale. So, it petrified me, as a loner, to be situated amongst a hundred other children who were all, much to my horror, taller than me.

A lanky brunette wearing black leggings and a skull-adorned pink tunic stood in front of me, clutching her backpack to her chest and talking to herself, or so I assumed. I'd cast a glare of betrayal back at my parents, who both waved and smiled encouragingly. At that moment, I hated them for their treachery. I'd been happy at home in my own little Lily bubble, and the fact that they were making me go out in the world to face other people felt royally unfair.

"Stop that," I heard the girl in front of me say. "No, you have to stay inside."

I personally thought she was nutty as a walnut tree.

She glanced over her shoulder at me and said, "Your hair matches Tizzy's."

I thought she was insulting me until a tiny head popped out of the backpack, and the small red squirrel said, "*Letmesee*, Haze!"

And in those few seconds of meeting my soon-to-be future BFF and her exuberant flying-squirrel familiar, I no longer felt abandoned and stranded.

So when Parker offered me his hand to shake, I took it. "Nice to meet you. I'm Lily."

"Are you all right, Miss Mason?" asked the mechanic Greer Knowles. He strolled quickly toward Parker and me. For an older gentleman, he moved with ease.

"Yes." I put my mittens back on because between the cold wind and Smooshie's saliva, a patch of ice was forming on my palms. "Thanks."

"That damn four-way is going to get someone killed."

"Morning, Dad," Parker said. Apparently, the nice-smelling dog rescuer was the mechanic's son. "You know the council is never going to approve the money for a stop sign."

"They will when someone dies." Greer shook his head and turned his attention to me. "Good news. You sheared the distributor. Bad news, the part I need to fix your car is in Oklahoma. It will be Tuesday before it gets here."

"How much?"

"Forty-eight for the part, plus twenty-five labor."

It was a fair price. More than fair, but I couldn't help but think about the chunk it would eat out of my savings, especially since I didn't have a job. Every cent I had would need to last me.

"Thanks," I said. Smooshie contented herself to stay

next to me, and I admit, having her close made me feel more calm and centered. She was better than a mood stone.

"I've rarely seen a dog so taken with someone right from the get-go," Parker said. "You want to come down to the rescue and fill out the paperwork?"

"Sure," I said. I had nowhere to live. Which meant, the dog was going to be just as homeless as I was right now. Jeez, I hadn't thought this through.

"Uhm, Parker."

"Yeah."

"I'm just visiting family for a couple of days. I don't even have a place to stay yet. I doubt if a B&B will let me keep Smooshie. Can you keep her for a couple more days?"

Parker smiled. "I have a studio apartment over my garage. It's just a bed, a bathroom, and a kitchenette, but you're welcome to it as long as you need it."

"It'll only be two or three days at the most."

He waved me off. "However long."

"You don't even know me."

"You're kind, Lily. I can tell in the way you are with Smooshie. As far as I'm concerned, that's all I need to know."

"Parker!" a woman shouted. "Parker Knowles!" I looked up to see Katherine Kapersky sprinting toward us. She looked ready to spit nails. For such a put-together woman, she had an attitude worse than a skunk Shifter's. And they were as crotchety as shapeshifters come.

Parker groaned. "Not now," he said out the side of his mouth.

"That woman needs a muzzle more than your dogs," Greer said. "You better get, son."

"Come on," Parker said to me. "My place is just three streets down." He didn't bother waiting for me to answer as he headed in the opposite direction of my uncle's café. Smooshie and I were right on his tail.

So was Mrs. Kapersky.

"Parker!" The woman used his name like a demand. "I know you can hear me."

I looked back over my shoulder. Her blonde hair had enough hair spray that it barely moved, even with her brisk pace. She flapped her pocketbook in our direction.

"I think she's going to follow you all the way to the shelter."

"Probably," Parker said. He stopped and turned. "Mrs. Kapersky. So nice to see you." Even though his words had been meant as a polite kindness, I could taste the lie like a green persimmon's bitterness on my tongue, an unfortunate side effect of my witch inheritance.

"I saw that dog of yours running around the streets." Her finger shook as she pointed it at him. "Between your beasts and the crazy drivers, this town is turning dangerous for folks to even walk around in."

Had she seen my near miss with the car, or had she had a close encounter of her own?

The creases between Parker's eyes deepened. "My dogs have never hurt anyone, and you know it."

"The board meets this week, and I promise you, we will be voting on whether to ban the shelter from the city limits."

"Mrs. Kapersky." Parker's body went rigid, his hands flexing as if self-control was something he had to practice. "This is Lily Mason. She's adopting the dog right now. You won't have to worry about her anymore."

"Too little too late," the woman snapped.

Parker's dad was right behind her. "If you want a real cause, Katie, you'd get this sign fixed. Miss Mason here almost got ran over."

The woman turned her laser beam eyes to the mechanic. "You stay out of this, Greer." And with that, she turned on her heel and stormed off.

Parker shook his head.

His dad said, "That woman was born in a briar patch and never got all the thorns out of her sorry hide."

"That's no lie," Parker agreed.

"I'm glad you're okay, Miss Mason," Greer said.

I nodded at him. "Thanks."

"All right." He gestured toward his son, who was already heading off again. "Parker's a good kid. He'll take care of you. I'll give him a call when the truck is ready." The scowl on his face returned as he stared down the street at the Kapersky woman. "Have a nice day, Miss Mason."

It took a minute to catch up with Parker. Smooshie, who'd been silent during Mrs. Kapersky's tirade, whined. Her sad gaze made me want to go werecougar on the horrid woman. I know it had only been five minutes, but Smooshie was under my protection now. Anyone foolish enough to be mean to her would find my claws in their behind.

"What was that all about?" I asked.

Parker scratched behind her ear. "It's nothing for you to worry about," he said. "She's an old witch."

Alarm rang through me. A witch was responsible for the deaths of my parents and my brother. While I knew they weren't all bad, my best friend Haze, for example, I also knew that a rogue witch could cause a lot of damage and chaos. "A witch? How old?" The older ones tended to be more powerful, and as wrinkly as she looked, she had to be a thousand years or more.

"I'm pretty sure the crone celebrated her sixtieth birthday last year."

"Only sixty?" I tucked my chin. She couldn't have strong magic. I was still getting used to my own witch DNA, and I didn't really have a hold on my own power yet. The blonde hair marked Mrs. Kapersky as a creator. "Do you have many…witches living in Moonrise?"

"We have our share, just like anywhere else."

Really? It surprised me that he would know about witches. I was certain this was a human-only town, with the exception of my uncle. Hazel, now the chief of police in my hometown of Paradise Falls, had lived in the human world for nearly two decades, and no one had been the wiser. She said it was pretty easy to hide. But she'd been a witch, not a Shifter, and I wondered if it was easier to hide magic than shifting.

"Does she have a coven?" I asked.

Parker raised his brow at me. "A what?"

"Mrs. Kapersky. I just wondered if she had a coven because I don't sense her magic."

"If by magic, you mean pure meanness, then yeah. That woman is a demon."

Was she a witch or a demon? I was lost. Surely, Uncle

Buzz would have mentioned if paranormal beings lived here.

He studied me. "I don't mean she's a real witch. She likes to complain about everything all the time and stir up trouble."

Oh. I blushed. He wasn't talking about real witches. Duh. "I think the word you're looking for starts with a B. I've known a few of those, too. Ironic she's married to the preacher."

"No doubt."

The rescue shelter smelled nicer than I thought it would. I mean, it definitely smelled like dog, but when you housed a bunch of dogs, that couldn't be helped.

"How many do you have?"

"Right now I have enough room to take care of twenty dogs, but only enough volunteers for about eight. I'm trying to save enough to buy some property outside of town. I want to build a large shelter on at least ten acres to house at least two hundred dogs." He shook his head. "I hate having to turn away a pit bull that needs care and attention. Some of them come to me in pretty bad shape."

I hated to think of what Smooshie must have gone through before her rescue. "Do you take care of them by yourself?"

"I have two employees and some volunteers. Good

folks who will come and hang out with the dogs in care, re-socialize them to people. When they are ready, we have foster homes who keep them until we can get them adopted. Like with children, it takes a village. We get donations in from all over the state, money, food, and such. The local vet office, Petry's Pet Clinic, vaccinates the dogs for free, and neuters and spays them for me."

"That's really nice of the vet."

"Ryan Petry is an old buddy. I usually ask for a small adoption fee from prospective owners. What I get, I give to Ryan. It covers his costs for the medicines."

"How do you keep it going? I mean, if you give away the adoption fees?"

He chuckled. "The rest of this place is paid for with donations from animal lovers all over the state. We have regular monthly and one-time donors. It's not a lot, but it keeps the lights on." He smiled. "We have a website people can access."

His love for the breed moved me. "That's really wonderful. These dogs are lucky to have you in their corner."

"I'd do anything to keep them safe."

I hadn't had much help when I was raising my brother. Maybe if I had, he wouldn't have died so young. "It's a noble endeavor."

He smiled. "The dogs help me as much as I help them."

He didn't elaborate, so I didn't pry.

"Thanks for putting me up," I said, trying real hard not to move in closer for a better whiff of his delicious scent. "I won't be a bother. I don't plan to stay in town long."

Parker's blue eyes softened. "That's too bad."

CHAPTER 4

The room over Parker's garage had a bathroom with a shower, a small kitchenette with a sink, a microwave, two electric burners, and a small oven. The cabinets were shallow and few, so not a lot of storage. The refrigerator was small, maybe twenty-four inches wide with a small freezer up top. The fridge part was stocked with beer and pop, and the freezer had two bags of ice. Parker had shrugged apologetically when he'd shown me but told me to help myself. I had planned to go back to The Cat's Meow for dinner, but Parker offered to cook me spaghetti. It wasn't my favorite meal, but I found it difficult to say no to him.

Smooshie claimed an old recliner as her throne, curling to fill the entire seat. I'd set out a pan of water while I waited for Parker to come back with some food for her. I sat on the edge of the loveseat, which pulled out into a bed, and stared at the sparsely furnished place. The dog had rolled over onto her back, and the tip of her tongue was perilously close to touching her eyeball.

Suddenly, I was overwrought with the impending responsibility of dog ownership. I couldn't keep my family alive. What the heck made me think I could keep Smooshie alive? Why in the world had I left Paradise Falls? I had a home there, even if the bank had owned it. I'd had a life, even if it hadn't been the one I'd always dreamed of. I'd wanted to be a doctor at one time.

Now I was in Moonrise with an uncle who didn't want me around, a dog who needed me around, and a man who took the breath right out of me whenever he was around.

A knock startled me from my reverie.

Parker opened the door and peeked his head in. "May I come in?"

"Sure," I told him. He wasn't wearing his big coat now, just a dark-blue flannel shirt that made his eyes shine like sapphires. Man, did he smell good. Even over the scent of the bagged dog food he carried inside.

He nodded at Smooshie and smiled. "I see she's settling in."

"Seems so," I said. I hoped I could be as adaptable.

"You okay?" he asked.

"Don't I look okay?"

"You look…sad."

"Well, I'm not." I stood up and got a bowl from one of the cabinets. The whole chair rattled when Smooshie leaped from it and scrabbled over. Parker sidled up next to me, and the overwhelming scent of honey and mint, like a wintery perfume, overwhelmed my senses. Goddess, this guy had a strange effect on me.

He dished out two large scoops of food into the bowl, and Smooshie went to town.

"Were you starving, girl?" I scratched her butt and cast an unwarranted, but accusatory gaze at Parker. "When was the last time she ate?"

"I like that you're already protective over her."

Quit being so reasonable. He was making it hard to ignore him. Truth was, Smooshie didn't look like she missed too many meals. Like ever.

He handed me a leash.

"She'll need to go out in about an hour or two. But watch it if she gets whiney or fidgety before then. She hasn't pooped since this morning."

"That you know of." I focused on the pit bull. "She did get loose from you."

"You're right," he agreed. "Just giving you fair warning. The land behind the shelter is fenced-in, you can take her out there to do her business. It will give her a chance to run as well. Careful, though. She's a digger. That's how she got out earlier."

"I will make a note of it."

He put his hand on my shoulder, forcing me to meet his gaze. "I'll have the spaghetti ready about five-thirty. Is that too early?"

"Nope." I licked my dry lips and reminded myself that I wasn't looking for romance, and certainly not with a human. There were things about me that would be too hard to explain. Like the fact that there were times I had more fur than the dogs he rescued. "I'll be there."

His small house was next to the garage. The shelter was on the other side. He had about two acres of backyard. When he'd taken me on the tour, I could see why he wanted more land for his dogs. It was just going on two in the afternoon now, which meant, I had a little time before dinner.

Parker's dad ran my luggage over, and I dug a pair of jeans out of my suitcase and changed from my torn leggings. It was after lunch now, so probably the perfect time to have a conversation with Buzz.

"Well, Smooshie." I hooked the leash on her collar. A difficult feat, considering her whole body squirmed with excitement. "How do you feel about an adventure?"

She answered enthusiastically with a high-pitched yip.

"I thought you might like that."

THE WALK TO THE CAT'S MEOW CAFÉ WAS A SERIES OF Smooshie pulling and me holding her back. I was definitely going to have to have a long talk with her about walking etiquette. She had to weigh at least fifty pounds, and she was all muscle.

Just up ahead, near the café, Katherine Kapersky strolled toward me. She was on the phone, her face red and her tone harsh. An argument of some kind, I surmised. I crossed to the other side of the road with Smooshie to give her a wide birth.

Mrs. Kapersky stopped when she noticed me, and said very loudly, "You curb that dog, you hear, or I'll make sure you're fined."

"Yes, ma'am." I kept my head down and finished the short walk to my uncle's business. I wondered if I could ask Haze to cast a curse on the old bitty. Okay, I wouldn't actually do that. But I'd known people like Katherine Kapersky my whole life, and she could really use a boil on her rear end.

When I was six years old, my parents took me to an Election Day event in Paradise Falls. Council members were being chosen for the Witch-Shifter Coalition. There would be three witches and three Shifters elected to sit on the board and broker conflicts between the two paranormal groups. My father had been one of the candidates, and I remember feeling enormous pride at the way people looked at him, the respect they used when they spoke to him, and the support he received from the *Felidae*, or big cat Shifters in our community.

At one point in the evening, one of the werecougars, a Maureen Hobart, strolled up to my father, and I was certain she would shake his hand. Instead, she looked down at me, disgust apparent in her sneer.

"If you can't do any better than produce runt offspring then you have no business leading our people."

My stomach dropped as I received the full extent of her vitriol. Her hateful comment made me wonder if I was defective. I learned, at that moment, that there were people who had a gift for making other people feel small, a knack for cruelty that sliced fast and deep.

My mother's response was swift. She punched Maureen in the face. "Keep your mouth shut, or I'll rip out your vocal chords, and you'll never speak again."

That's when I learned that sometimes bullies picked on the wrong people and got their spiteful derrieres handed to them. My father's way of handling disputes tended to be more on the peace, love, and under-standing side, but my mother had been a fierce and unapologetic protector.

I missed them so much.

Smooshie and I reached the diner and went inside. The toasty heat felt wonderful. Buzz and Freda sat in the corner booth, rolling silverware into napkins. I knew Buzz had heard me before I entered, but Freda jumped a little in surprise. She got up and smiled at me.

"Sorry, hon, there are no dogs allowed in here." Her tone was apologetic.

My uncle stood up and patted Freda on the shoulder. "It's okay, Freed. It's not like we have anyone in here to complain."

"All right." Freda gestured to the empty diner. "Sit anywhere you like, hon."

WHILE FREDA BUSIED HERSELF ELSEWHERE IN THE CAFÉ, Buzz and I sat in a booth closer to the front of the diner. Smooshie had lain down on the floor, put her head on her paws, and fallen asleep. Every so often she'd let out a snore or a snuffle.

Two minutes with Buzz Mason, and I'd learned one important thing: The man could charm sugar off an ant's back.

"So your truck needs some work, eh?"

"Yep. Poor Martha crapped out on me the second I got to town."

"Huh. Fate must want you to stick around then."

This from the man who'd told me not to stay? "I don't believe in fate."

"I do," he said. His smile was open, friendly, and so much like Danny's that it made my chest hurt.

"I wished you'd been able to meet my younger brother," I said. "He was killed last year." I couldn't meet Buzz's eyes. "Murdered. By the same people who'd killed my parents."

"I'm so sorry, Lily." He reached over and patted the top of my hand. I appreciated the small gesture of comfort.

"You would've loved Danny."

Buzz's mouth dropped, his eyes wide and unblinking. "Danny?"

"Short for Daniel."

"They named their son after me?" He took that in, looking shell-shocked. Sorrow edged into his gaze. "All those years gone because of my pride. I'm a damned fool."

"What's done is done," I said, repeating one of my dad's favorite phrases. "My parents never mentioned you, Buzz. I didn't know you existed until a month ago." I put my elbows on the table. "What happened? How did you and my dad grow so far apart?"

"You know. It's classic boy-meets-girl, girl-falls-for-boy's-older-brother. Your mom and I were the same age and shared some classes in high school." He smiled wistfully. "I'd loved her for as long as I could remember. But then your mother told me Jack smelled like pinecones and pumpkins. And he said that she smelled like butterscotch and whipped cream." He shook his head. "Shifters can't resist the mating scent. That primal response can't be denied, no matter what. I understood that, but I couldn't watch the woman I loved mate with my brother. I left Paradise Falls, and that was that."

"Did you ever think about coming back?"

Buzz nodded. "Plenty of times, but I always talked myself out of it. Then it had been so long since I'd been home that I didn't see the point of interrupting Jack and Constance's life together. We didn't part on the best of terms." He swallowed hard. "I can't believe he's been gone all these years. I always imagined he and Constance were having this wonderful life."

"They did up until the day they died." I'd always felt safe with them. Loved. "Danny was seven when they were taken from us. I was barely eighteen."

Buzz's hand covered mine. "You've lost a lot."

"We both have." I wiped my face with the back of my hand. "I've never lived around humans before. Any pointers to get me by for the next couple of days?"

"Pretend you don't see, hear, or smell as much stuff as you do. It weirds humans out."

I laughed. "Good tip."

"Oh, and if any parakind stuff is brought up, just pretend like it's all fiction. I love being around humans. They are wonderfully complicated, but they're clueless about the supernatural, and if you want to keep your secrets, you have to act just as clueless." Buzz chuckled, his eyes settling on me. "You look a lot like your mom, Lily."

"Scrawny?"

"Beautiful."

I warmed at his compliment. "Thanks."

"I have to get to prepping dinner. It starts getting busy in here after four on Sunday. Come back for an evening meal?"

"Parker Knowles is going to fix me some spaghetti."

"He is, is he?"

"It's just dinner, Buzz."

He leaned close, almost conspiratorially. "It's never just dinner, Lily."

I HAD A COUPLE OF HOURS BEFORE I WAS SUPPOSED TO BE at Parker's, so I wandered around town a little with Smooshie. I'd grabbed a few white bags from Buzz, just in case I ran into that woman again.

I could hear a chorus of voices singing something about

the Holy Ghost and allowed Smooshie to lead me in that direction. The sidewalk had been stained with salt, but at least it wasn't slick. Good thing, because the way the dog was dragging me along, any ice would have landed me on my backside.

Pretty soon we were on the steps of a church built on a large corner lot. The singing was melodic and the harmonies decent. I'm no expert, but with my hearing, I could tell some singers were better than others. I went up the steps. The door was unlocked, so I went inside. My understanding of human religion was that all were welcome. I hoped it was true of dogs as well, because I wasn't leaving Smooshie outside.

"Stop. Just stop," I heard a shrill voice say as we stepped inside the entrance area.

I groaned. Not again. Katherine Kapersky. Did the woman have an evil clone factory? That would explain why she was seemingly everywhere.

I stood under the arch that separated the entrance from the fellowship hall. The Kapersky woman stood up on a stage at the back of the church with a choir of five women and three men who faced her. She wore a blue wraparound dress and pointed a finger at a young beachy-blonde in the front row who practically quivered under the scrutiny.

"If you can't reach the F, Bridgette, you might find yourself out of a solo." She snapped her fingers. "Now, tighten it up. No more cracking on the high notes."

The perky blonde's face darkened, but she didn't say a word. Kapersky gestured to the pianist, and the chorus of voices started the song from the beginning.

A woman with dark hair, her blue eyes hard with anger and her mouth grimly set, entered the church behind me. Her arm brushed mine as she shoved past. I could smell lilacs and vodka on her, and the scent of a new baby. She either had an infant at home, or she babysat for one. I hoped she didn't watch the kid when drinking the vodka.

Rex Kapersky, the minister, saw her and nodded. He pointed to a door on the right side of the stage. The woman nodded and glanced back once, tears cresting her eyes, before the two of them went inside.

I watched as Katherine, her expression curious and worried, expertly noted the entire exchange without missing a musical beat.

CHAPTER 5

Being from the north, I had a great pair of winter boots, water-proofed and fleece-lined. Shifters aren't immune to the cold, especially not in human form, but Smooshie and I moved at a brisk walk. Between the boots and my wool coat, I didn't suffer much.

Smooshie tried to dig up an evergreen bush, a mailbox, and a stop sign as we walked. And stopped. And walked. She pooped twice, and recalling Katherine Kapersky's shrill warning, I picked it up. I wondered if Smooshie would be willing to dig a hole to bury her own poop. Carrying around another animal's feces, even in a plastic bag, was a new and disturbing experience.

We passed a VFW hall, a hardware store, a pharmacy, and a Walmart Supercenter. I'd looked up Moonrise before making the decision to come here. According to the internet, it had a population of 18,576. Not a city, by any means, but large enough that it had a community college. I don't know why it surprised me that it felt so roomy and spread out. Paradise Falls was minuscule by comparison.

By the time we made it back to Parker's house, it was after five, and I was tired and cold. So was Smooshie.

"Get inside," he said when he opened the door. "You're growing icicles off your nose."

Automatically, I put my fingers to my nose. No icicles. Ah. Dang it. I really needed to get used to a human's propensity for exaggeration. Luckily, Parker took my coat and didn't seem to notice my faux pas. I stared at his big biceps and his wide chest. I come from a town where some of the men are seven feet tall, but Parker wasn't that tall. Still, I'm short, especially for a Shifter, and I still had to look up to see his face.

"Thanks," I said.

"You're welcome."

"The spaghetti smells good." Not that I could smell it particularly well over his aroma. Once again, I was overwhelmed by the pleasant scent of honey and mint.

"I hope you like a meat sauce."

"The meatier, the better." I do turn into a pure carnivore some of the time, and we cats like our meat.

"It's my mom's recipe. She was Italian."

"Was?"

"She died when I was in high school."

"I'm sorry." I understood his loss all too well. "I lost my folks my senior year."

"Still fresh, huh?" He shook his head. "It doesn't get better, but it gets easier."

"It was a while ago," I said. "I'm okay now."

He gave me an odd look. "You can't be more than twenty or twenty-one."

I smiled, startled at his observation. I couldn't tell him that I was closer to forty than twenty. As my uncle said, I had to blend. "Yeah, uh…" I scrambled to think of an appropriate age. I went for ten years past high school. "Actually, I'm twenty-eight."

"Wow, you look much younger."

"I'll take that as a compliment," I told him.

He laughed. "I'm twenty-five, and I feel older than dirt."

"Well, you look great." I grinned. "For dirt." Was I flirting? Noooo. I couldn't flirt. *He is a human. I am a Shifter,* I reminded myself. *This is not a date. I am only visiting.*

A large dog, even bigger than Smooshie, with the most beautiful silvery-blue fur, lay quietly in the corner of the kitchen. He was obviously an American pit bull mix. I think the other half of him was horse.

Smooshie slid across the floor to the dog and enthusiastically started sniffing his butt. "Smoosh!" I chastised. She unceremoniously ignored me and kept her examination going for a couple more seconds before Parker shooed her off.

He reached down and patted the giant dog's head. "This here is Elvis."

"I thought he left the building."

Parker's blue eye's twinkled. "He's a hunka-hunka burning love."

"I can see that." I kneeled down and let Elvis sniff my hand. "Is he a rescue too?"

"Sorta." Parker held out a chair for me. Such a gentleman. "The truth is that he rescued me."

"That must be a dog thing." My brown-and-white girl put her head in my lap and looked at me with those liquid brown eyes. Once again, I felt my heart melting. "Such a good girl," I told her. Her tail played a staccato rhythm on the table leg.

"Elvis is gorgeous." *Like you*, I wanted to blurt. "What's he mixed with?"

"Great Dane."

Smooshie jumped up, practically throwing herself across my lap. Her enthusiasm knocked over the chair next to me, and she scrambled under the table to hide. Poor baby. I didn't like to see her so skittish, and I wondered what her life had been like before Parker had taken her in. I got up and set the chair to rights. Smooshie grinned at me from underneath the table, but she didn't come out. I sat back down and glanced at Elvis. "He didn't even flinch. He's really laid-back."

Parker reached under the table and scratched Smooshie's back. "Elvis has a chill personality, but he's also had a lot of training."

I opened my mouth to ask about the training, but Parker's closed expression had me swallowing my question. Elvis seemed as laid-back as Parker. He was a patient man. I found I really liked that about him. Even with the white lie he'd told that woman earlier about it being nice to see her, my witchy-truth senses told me he was inherently an honest man. My Shifter hormones didn't particularly care if the guy was noble or not, as long as he kept looking and smelling good, but I was trying to ignore them at the moment.

"Is it okay if I make you a plate?" he asked.

"Sure."

He piled two bowls with spaghetti noodles and sauce. He finished them off by putting toasted garlic bread on the side. He set mine in front of me and handed me a fork and a napkin.

"Do you want tea, water, beer, or wine?"

"Let's get crazy. How about a beer?"

"Domestic or foreign?"

"Domestic."

"Whew," he said. "It's all I have."

"What if I'd asked for foreign?"

"The liquor store is just a couple of blocks down. Not even a five-minute round trip."

I laughed. The spaghetti noodles were long and twirled easily around my fork. "This looks really good." I shoved the whole bundle into my mouth. It was the best spaghetti I'd ever eaten. "I'll never eat sauce from a jar again," I said after I swallowed. I licked the corner of my mouth, enjoying the tang. "So good."

Parker's eyes lit with pleasure as he watched me eat. "I'm glad you think so."

There was an uncomfortable lull of silence, so I blurted out, "That reverend's wife is a real piece of work."

"You don't know the half of it."

"Do tell." I took another bite and chewed while I waited for him to dish.

"She's got half the town out of their minds. She's advocating for a new chain restaurant that has made a few restaurant owners angry, she won't do anything about the dangerous missing stop sign by my dad's, and she's trying to get pit bulls banned from town."

"Can she do that?"

"Missouri has a breed ban law, so yes, if she gets enough votes, she can." He shook his head, his expression pinched, and his body tensed up. Elvis popped to his massive feet and padded next to his human. The big dog leaned into Parker's thigh. Parker put his hand on Elvis' head, closed his eyes and took a breath. He exhaled slowly and then opened his eyes. "Her own brother, Ed Miles, can't stand her. She has so many people scared in town."

"Even you?"

The corner of his mouth tugged up. "I'm not scared of her, but I wouldn't put anything past her. It's gonna be a real fight once she officially sets her sights on my shelter. Right now, though, Katherine Kapersky has bigger fish to fry than me." He ate a bite of food. "I hear there is a new church being built outside of the city limits."

I used my fork to gesture. "I saw several churches in town. Why is another one such a big deal?"

"It's the same denomination as her husband's church. Some of the Rev's flock have already abandoned Sunday services. Once there's an alternative, I wouldn't be surprised if every one of his parishioners changed where they worshiped."

I didn't quite understand the approach humans took to honoring their deity. From what I understood, most everyone seemed to believe in one God. Why there were different rituals and expectations in worshipping didn't make sense to me. I remembered how Katherine had admonished her brother for not being in church that morning. If her idea of keeping the pews filled included intimidation and meanness, I could see why people would prefer a Katherine-free zone.

"The Rev is a nice enough guy, but he's clueless when it comes to his wife. Not only is she driving away his flock, she uses her power as the president of the town council to make people's lives miserable." He shook his head in disbelief. "I still don't know how that happened. My dad used to be on the council. He says it was more than her charm that got her elected."

I scooted forward. "What does that mean?"

Parker laughed. "You know I haven't talked this much in a year. It's nice talking to you."

I felt a blush heat my face. I knew my witch talent played a part in Parker opening up to me, but still, the compliment made me happy. "Thanks."

The conversation veered away from Katherine. Parker told me more about Moonrise, and I told him about surprising my "cousin" with an unexpected visit. Then he talked about his stint in the Army, though he didn't go into too much detail. Before I knew it, three hours had passed, but with Parker, it had felt like five minutes.

For Smooshie, it felt longer, because she raced to the back door when I stood up and barked, her butt, not just her tail, wagging vigorously.

"I think someone needs to go out," Parker said. Elvis perked his head up then stood and trotted to the door to stand with Smoosh. "Two someones."

"It was nice of them to wait until the evening ended."

"Yes," Parker said. His eyes crinkled as he smiled. "It was really nice of them."

We put on our coats and let the dogs out. Parker's covered back porch stretched to the end of his house. He had a wheelbarrow with remnants of hay near the door, two tubs of dog toys, and a baseball bat.

"Looking to start an all-dog team?" I asked as I picked up the bat. It was wooden, a real slugger, with a nicely hefty weight. I walked to the edge of the porch and gave it a swing. "Nice."

"Wow, you handle that like a pro."

"I played a little when I was younger." Even Shifters and witches weren't immune to the lure of sporty competitions. My size usually got me picked last for a team, but still, those warm summer days hitting balls and running bases were some of my best memories.

He took the bat from me. "You've got a nice swing." He set it down next to the door. "I used to play too. I was scouted by a few colleges before I decided on the military. Now, I use it to scare off foxes and coyotes who come inside the fence."

I knew a few foxes and coyotes back home who'd take

real offense at having a bat shook at them. They were mostly jerks, so I wasn't offended in the least. "I bet you get some scavengers over here." Smooshie finished her business and the time was getting late. "I've had such a nice evening, Parker."

"I hope we can do it again before you go back home." Parker's gaze made my belly flutter, and for a moment, I wanted him to kiss me.

No. No. Nope. I couldn't ignore my uncle's advice. I didn't have enough experience around humans to be sure I could avoid revealing my true self. And Parker made me the most jittery.

"I'd love to hang out again," I said.

Parker walked us through the house to the front door. With a final goodbye, Smooshie and I headed to the outdoor stairs that led to the garage.

THE HIGH-PITCHED WHIMPERING WOKE ME FROM MY restless sleep. I'd been tossing and turning since I hit the sheets a little after ten o'clock. I rolled over and grabbed my phone from the end table. The digital display revealed it was only 12:06 a.m. A wet tongue poked inside my ear, and I sat up. "Ugh, Smoosh. No wet willies, okay?"

She planted her paws on my chest and rested her head

on top. She woofed softly. By the way she squirmed, I'd say she'd woken up with a full bladder.

I dressed quickly, the dog nudging me with her shoulder and whacking me with her tail the whole time. I smiled. It was really nice having someone to care for. I'd taken care of my younger brother for so long it had been strange to not have anyone to nurture anymore. His loss had created a hole so big, I'd never been able to fill it. Since meeting Smooshie, though, I'd felt needed again. I clipped her leash to her collar, and we headed out.

The gate to the backyard creaked as we went through. I locked it behind me, and I let Smooshie go. A bright quarter moon hung in the cloudless sky, its soft light making the snow look blue. A blast of bitter cold forced me to huddle into my coat. Smooshie trotted off, seemingly oblivious to the freezing temperature.

She sniffed around for a minute, then her head went up, and she took off toward the back fence. I saw her examining something near the chain link and then she started issuing high-pitched yips. I started trotting toward her making shushing noises. "You're gonna wake up the entire block."

Another gust of sharp wind chilled me to the bone, but the scent of blood—human blood—was what really froze me. "Smooshie," I hissed. "Smooshie! Get over here."

Smooshie returned to me, and I clipped her back on the

leash. Keeping a firm hand on the leash, I moved forward.

From almost fifty feet away, I could make out a person-sized shape lying in the snow. I swallowed hard as my gorge rose. I smelled body waste mixed in with the coppery scent of blood. Smooshie whined, letting me know she'd scented it, too.

For a split second, I worried that the crumpled figure was Parker. My heart raced as adrenaline put my senses on high alert. As I soon as I got close enough, I realized the body was too small to be Parker.

New girl in town finds the corpse of town hag. Panic welled inside me. Crap. Crap. Carp. What was it with me and death? I'd driven 700 miles to get away from murderers and their victims, and here I was on Day One, faced with a deceased human.

I wanted to run the other way, but Haze would be ashamed of me if I acted like a Chicken McChick-enpants.

The victim was planted face down in the freezing white powder, her yellow-blonde hair fanned out like wispy octopus tentacles across the blood-stained snow.

My stomach soured.

Hints of rose and woody fragrance filtered through the more odious aromas. I recognized the scent. Without seeing the dead woman's face, I knew this was Katherine Kapersky, scourge of Moonrise, Missouri.

"Stay put," I told Smooshie, and, surprisingly, she listened. I took off a glove and shoved it in my pocket. The light stench of sweet, decomposing flesh, even at this early stage, told me she was dead. Still, I felt for a pulse. Nothing. I could still feel the cold sponginess of her skin on my fingertips even after I stopped touching her.

I inhaled deeply to see if I could catch any other scent. Beneath her cloying perfume, I detected the faint whiff of beef liver and onions, some kind of alcohol, cloves, and mint. Gently, I turned her head toward me. I didn't want to disturb evidence, but I wanted to get a better whiff of the liquor on her breath. It was familiar, but I didn't know why. Maybe a gin of some kind?

My gaze dropped to the right side of her face. There was a weird bruising pattern, three circular bruises, on her jaw. I was tempted to turn her head the other way, but I'd already messed with the crime scene enough.

I noticed then that Katherine wasn't wearing gloves. It was below freezing outside. Two broken nails on her right hand marred her perfect manicure.

I wished I could shift into my cougar form. My non-animal form had better senses than a human, but my cat form was even better at discerning individual scents. However, I wasn't in Paradise Falls anymore.

Smooshie put her nose to the dead woman's wrist, and I gently tugged her back.

The light from Parker's back porch came on. "What's going on out here?" he asked loudly.

Shoot. *Oh, hi, Parker. Smooshie needed to pee and by the way, ding, dong, the witch Katherine Kapersky is dead...in your backyard. Surprise!*

CHAPTER 6

I'd been around death enough that I didn't panic. I decided to call in the Cavalry. I tightened my grip on Smooshie's leash, intending to return to the house, but a silvery glint next to the body caught my eye. I squatted for a better look.

Mostly buried in the snow, the edge of the object gleamed. I put on my glove and picked up the item. It was an alligator clip. I'd found several in my brother's room after he died, along with a few mostly smoked marijuana cigarettes, aka roaches, and a one-hitter, its sides thick with pot resin. I'd been aware of his drug use, but he'd been an adult, and he was allowed to make his own choices.

I sniffed the clip. No dank earthy smell. Huh. I expected to get at least a vague marijuana scent, but there was nothing.

Was this important to Katherine's death? Or had some

kid dropped it back here? I couldn't be sure, so I dropped it back where I'd found it.

"Hey!" Parker stood at the edge of his porch holding his bat. "Who's back there?"

"It's me," I yelled. "Lily."

He jogged out to Smooshie and me, his boots loosely laced and his jacket unbuttoned. "What's going on?"

"Don't freak out."

His expression turned wary. "When people say don't freak out, it's because there's something to freak out about."

"I can't argue with your logic." I stepped back and turned, pointing to the corpse.

"Jesus Christ," he whispered, his voice suddenly hoarse, his breath quickening to a pant. Elvis nudged his big head under Parker's hand, and I heard Parker's breathing almost immediately slow down. The dog had an unbelievable calming effect on his friend. "Please don't tell me she was mauled by dogs."

"I really don't think a pit bull can wield a blunt object. Her head looks like a burst melon."

He paled. Elvis nudged him again.

"Sorry," I said. "That was too graphic."

"No. It's okay. I've seen worse." He glanced at Katherine's corpse. "I thought I'd gotten away from death after I left Afghanistan. But here it is in my own backyard."

"I'm sorry." I waited a beat. "I don't have my cell phone. Do you?"

Parker shook his head. "I'll call nine-one-one from the house."

"Okay." I handed him Smooshie's leash. "You take the dogs inside, and I'll wait with the body."

Parker's relief was almost palpable. I couldn't begin to imagine the horrors he'd witnessed as a soldier, or how those memories continued to haunt and hurt him.

Fifteen minutes later, three police cars and one volunteer firefighter truck parked along the sidewalk in front of Parker's place. They had come in sirens blaring, and I could see house lights going on down the street.

The first person on the scene introduced himself as Sheriff Mike Avery, a burly man with super short salt-and-pepper hair. He had deep squint lines around his eyes, full-on crevices in his forehead, and lips that dropped into a frown. He smelled like French fries, strawberry ice cream, malt, and…kale chips. He wore a green ball cap with Sheriff embroidered across the front and law enforcement emblems decorating the bill. It matched his green uniform pants. He pulled a pen and small notebook from the pocket of his black winter coat.

"Miss Masters…"

"Mason," I corrected him. "Mason."

"Yes," he said, his mouth puckering as if he'd eaten something sour. "What were you doing out here in the middle of the night?"

I resisted the urge to say, "I was really hoping to find a dead body. And look, I found a doozy." Instead, I said, "I'd come out with Smooshie—"

"Who is Smooshie?" he interrupted, his voice suspicious.

"She's my dog," I said, surprising myself with how easy it was to stake my claim. I'd barely known her a day, but I already felt like she'd always been mine.

He made a tight-lipped "uh-huh" noise. "So you brought the dog out here for what purpose?"

I stared at him, but his serious gaze never wavered. Once again, I found myself biting my tongue to prevent a sarcastic comment. I sighed. "She needed to pee. Maybe poop. I don't know which."

"Uh-huh." Avery's heavy brows furrowed, two hairy commas highlighting deep-set eyes. I think his default expression must be set on "disapproval." He scribbled in his notebook. What clue could he possibly derive from a dog's bathroom habits? Did he plan to question my dog about doing Number One or Number Two?

I looked across the yard at Parker, who was being interviewed by another police officer. Parker had his arms crossed, his eyes narrowed with anger, his body bristling with annoyance. I wanted to go to him, to reassure him, but that was stupid. Just like the dog and this town, I barely knew the man. One meal didn't make us close. Hell, it didn't even make us friends.

"Miss Mason." I heard my name and a strident tapping. Sheriff Avery was tapping his pen against his notepad. When I refocused my attention on him, he looked at me then looked at Parker then back to me. "What is your relationship with Parker Knowles?"

"So far, he's given me temporary shelter and made me the best spaghetti I've ever had."

"Uh-huh." He flipped a page and then I watched the pen scratch across the paper.

"Do you know how to spell spaghetti?" I asked. I rose up on my tiptoes and tried to get a look at his notes.

He moved back, clucking his tongue. "You don't want to be charged with obstruction of justice, do you?"

My shoulders slumped. "What else do you need to know?"

"Are you sure Parker was in the house when you discovered Mrs. Kapersky?"

"Well, he wasn't in the backyard. It was just Smooshie and me." I jabbed a thumb at the body behind me. "And her."

The sheriff stared a hole right through me. "And you saw Parker with the bat?"

Suddenly wary, I nodded. Confirming that I'd seen him with the bat felt somehow like a betrayal.

"Are we almost done?" I asked. "I can't feel my fingers anymore."

"You seem in an awful hurry to get rid of me, Miss Mason."

Hell, yeah, I do. "If I stay out here much longer, you'll have a second body on your hands. It's twenty-five degrees outside, and I'm freezing."

"Uh-huh."

He put away the pen and notebook. "If you decide to move elsewhere in town, update my office with your new address. And Miss Mason…" He wrinkled his nose at me and sniffed. "Don't leave town."

"Wait. What? You think I'm a suspect?" I gaped at him. "Seriously?"

"Yep." Turning on the heel of his shiny, black boot, Sheriff Avery joined his deputy and Parker on the back porch. A man wearing a windbreaker over his winter coat that said "Coroner," approached me. I'd seen him poking around the body when the sheriff had pulled me aside. I guessed him to be in his mid-thirties. He had blond hair, light-brown eyes, and his frame was tall and thin. His black-rimmed glasses didn't fit well, and he kept adjusting them on his nose.

"How are you?" he asked.

"Pretty good, especially since I'm not the one who's dead."

He flashed a tepid smile. "It's unsettling to see a corpse."

I didn't tell him this wasn't my first crime scene. "Yeah, it's awful." I noticed then that he looked a little green. "You all right?"

He swallowed. Hard. "Don't think I'll ever get used to seeing dead bodies." He offered me a gloved hand. We shook. "I'm Tom Jones."

"Lily Mason," I said. "Tom Jones. Like the guy from Henry Fielding's novel."

"I usually get people naming the singer." He smiled, and it made me reassess his age. Maybe late twenties. "I like that you went for the classic."

"Thanks," I said. Tom the Coroner seemed like a decent guy. I couldn't detect any deceit in his scent, so I took a chance. "Did you notice the bruising on her face? It was weird."

"Bruising?"

"Three circular contusions, about an inch in diameter each on her right cheek, and they were blue." He had a blank expression, so I added, "The blue bruises means they happened a couple of hours before she died. Newer bruises are red."

He looked at me as if seeing me for the first time. "It was hard to get past all the blood on the back of her head."

Were all human doctors squeamish, or was it just him? It seemed an odd occupation to have if the sight of blood made you puke. "What is your medical background, Tom?"

"I'm an orthodontist," he answered.

A doctor for teeth? Really? I doubted Katherine died of explosive gingivitis. "So you're a dentist?"

"Orthodontist," he corrected.

"What's the difference?" I asked with genuine curiosity. Shifters didn't need dentists, usually, since we didn't get cavities. The occasional fight might cost us a tooth, but we had the ability to grow them back. If we didn't want to wait on nature, a witch healer could hurry things along.

"It's like the difference between a doctor who is a general practitioner and an endocrinologist. It's just a matter of specialty. Lots of braces and some cosmetic dentistry, though I do see regular patients as well."

Sooo, a dentist. "You're an orthodontist, and you're the coroner?"

"It's an elected position."

That explained it. Sorta. Not really. Humans were strange. Why would someone without an M.D. want to become a coroner? And why did humans vote on who got to do it? I didn't know how Haze or Uncle Buzz managed to assimilate in this upside-down, inside-out world.

"Don't worry. I'm sending Mrs. Kaspersky to a state-certified medical examiner." He chewed the left side of his lower lip. "Are you a doctor?"

"Gosh, no."

"A nurse?"

"I like to read a lot." I'd read anatomy and physiology books, the *Physician's Desk Reference* about pharmacology, and every differential diagnostic book I could get my hands on. My senior year, I'd been accepted to Iowa University, where I'd planned to get my premed degree. My parents' deaths had put an abrupt stop to my plans.

"I think she might have gotten into a physical fight. Maybe someone grabbed her face." I thought about how far back on the jaw the bruises were and looked at my own hands. "Someone strong enough to leave marks."

"Like Parker?"

I gave Tom a hard stare. "Parker had nothing to do with this."

He seemed a little taken aback by my assertion. "He's got military training. And everyone knows that he and Katherine had an ongoing dispute. No offense, but you haven't been in town long enough to make a judgment call."

I bristled. I was a Shifter and a witch, and my instincts were far better than his. "Are you investigating Parker?"

"Not me. My job is to decide if an investigation is warranted. And it is. My opinion is that this is a suspicious death." Tom eyed me. "And I think Parker had every reason in the world to beat Katherine to death."

CHAPTER 7

I tossed and turned for a couple of hours. Not even Smooshie's seesaw snores could lull me to sleep. I snuggled against her warm fur, glad that I didn't have to be in a strange place and a strange bed alone. I'd been so excited earlier. Moonrise had really started to feel like an adventure. Now it felt like a nightmare.

I pulled out my phone and dialed my best friend, Haze. It went straight to voice mail.

You've reached Police Chief Kinsey. If this is personal, leave a message. If somebody died, for the love of a horny squirrel, call the station. Don't forget to wait for the beep.

I didn't bother to wait. It was four in the morning, I'm sure she was sleeping, or, since she was a newlywed, otherwise occupied. Someone had died, but Moonrise wasn't in her jurisdiction. I had no doubt that Haze could investigate circles around the grumpy Sheriff Avery.

I stared at the ceiling counting the tiles as nervous energy rippled through me. So much so, my bones quivered with the desire to shift. Back home, it wouldn't have been a problem to change into my cougar form and go for a run, but around here I was certain someone would try to shoot me for being a dangerous wild animal.

I wanted this, right? I'd needed a change. The supernatural world is a difficult one to navigate if you aren't powerful or wealthy. I was neither. The point had been driven home when the police and the council in Paradise Falls had refused to investigate my brother's murder. For months, I had lived knowing that I was surrounded by people who couldn't give two shakes of a rat's ass about me. Haze had been FBI at the time, and she swooped in like a pro, and in two days managed to do what the town cops hadn't done in four months: catch the killers.

Smooshie's feet started kicking at me as her muzzle twitched, and she barked out the side of her mouth. Doggie dreams. I envied her ability to sleep.

My uncle Buzz told me he lived in a trailer behind the diner, and the longer I lay awake, the more I considered knocking on his door. He might not be able to help, but at least I didn't have to worry about giving myself away around him.

∾

SNOW FELL ACROSS THE STREET AND SIDEWALK, blanketing the area. The eerie quiet raised the hackles on my neck. I felt vulnerable. Alone.

My arm nearly jerked out of my socket, reminding me I wasn't by myself. Smooshie barked and tried to go after a squirrel—one without enough sense to hibernate for the winter.

"Stop that," I told her and pulled back on her leash. "You're going to wake the whole town."

She settled down but kept the leash tautly pulled in the direction of the squirrel. I smiled and thought of Tizzy, my BFF's familiar. She was a red flying squirrel with an unnerving flair for drama and fun. She also had the libido of a rabbit and could seduce another familiar in 1.2 seconds. I missed her like crazy.

Smooshie's tail whacked me a couple of times across the back of my knees as if to remind me that she wasn't chopped liver. I scratched behind her ear. "You're a good girl."

She wagged her whole body, her broad jaw cut into a wide grin. The frigid temperatures sank into my skin, and I questioned the sanity of leaving my warm bed. A few minutes later, we arrived at Buzz's diner and walked around to the back.

"There it is," I told Smooshie. I pointed ahead, not that she knew what the hell I was pointing at, and showed her Buzz's trailer. It was a twelve-by-sixty single-wide with white aluminum siding and green trim. It had to be an older model because the door looked like something you'd see on an RV, not on a home. A two-person metal rocker and tire, both covered in snow, were to the left of the stairs. A wind chime hung over the door. Its gentle tinkle as a light breeze blew against it felt more ominous than magical in the dead of night.

Smooshie climbed the two steps to the trailer door before me. She turned, her tail banging against the aluminum siding as she vibrated with excitement. "Calm down, girl."

The door opened before I could knock. "It's the middle of the night, Lily. What's going on?" Buzz asked.

"Katherine Kapersky is dead. I found her body," I blurted.

A brunette peeked her head out behind my uncle. I recognized her as Deputy Sheriff Nadine Booth. She was pulling on her pants and staggering sideways. "Did you call the police?" she said.

"Yes. They came and went."

She stopped fidgeting with her clothes. "Oh."

My uncle gave me side-eye. He backed up, and with a flourish of his hand, invited me and Smooshie inside his place.

"I should go," Deputy Booth said. She finished

buttoning her top and grabbed her coat. "I'll see you later, Buzz."

"You betcha," he told her as she hustled out the door without ceremony.

After she left, Buzz crossed his arms and gave me a stern look.

I shrugged. "I didn't mean to interrupt anything." Smooshie jumped onto his well-worn couch, an ugly thing made of woven orange, black, and brown wool. Frankly, it looked like the 1960s had curled up and died on it. Plus, it looked itchy and uncomfortable, but the dog seemed satisfied, as she flopped onto her belly and buried her head between two cushions. "Is that thing safe?"

"It's a couch. She'll be fine," Buzz said. He rubbed his thick fingers through his curly copper hair. "So Katie's dead." He blew out a breath. "That's going to stir up a hornet's nest around here."

"Murder has a way of doing that."

He raised a brow. "Murder?"

"The coroner is calling it a suspicious death." I found myself wanting a hug, but I didn't know Buzz well enough to embrace. I didn't want to make it awkward between us. "I found her in Parker's backyard. She was face down in the snow, and the back of her head was bashed in."

"I can't say I'm too surprised. She had her hooks into a number of people."

"Any of them want her dead?"

He pursed his lips. "It'd be easier to tell you who *didn't* want to kill her." Buzz walked into the tiny kitchenette and put a pot of coffee on. "Where did you say this happened?"

"Behind the Pit Bull Rescue Center."

"Kid finally snapped, eh? It was just a matter of time." Buzz shook his head. "He's been wired tighter than a bale of hay since he got back from the Army."

"I don't think Parker killed her."

"Now, Lily, humans aren't like us. He's got PTSD something bad. He served two tours over in Afghanistan. He was back stateside for almost a year before he moved back home with Elvis and opened his shelter."

"I don't know how to explain it." Other than my latent witch powers, which Buzz still didn't know about. "He made me dinner. He gave me a place to stay. He introduced me to Smooshie. All those are acts of a kind man."

"You might be right. All the same, Katherine's death will open a lot of wounds in this town. You might think about skedaddling before you get some blood on you."

"It wouldn't be the first time."

Buzz winced. "I'm really sorry about your mom and dad. About your brother." His eyes shimmered, and I noticed they were red-rimmed. I still felt my brother's death as if a part of me had been ripped away. Did Buzz feel that way about my dad? Was it possible to feel that kind of loss after forty years of no contact?

"You sure you're not letting your hormones get in the way of your common sense?"

I wasn't going to deny that I was attracted to Parker, but that had little to do with my belief he was innocent. Smooshie nudged her head underneath my hand as if she could sense the rise in my anxiety. I uncurled my fingers and stroked her fur. She put her chin on my lap. "You're a good girl," I told her.

"She's really taken with you," Buzz observed.

I was relieved at the swing in conversation. "The feeling is mutual." I gratefully accepted the cup of coffee my uncle offered.

He joined me at the small, two-person table.

"How do you do it?"

"What?"

"Live with humans and keep your secret?" I shook my head. "They aren't quiet enough to keep their private stuff private, they're unaware of how they smell, and they make a lot of eye contact, which feels like a challenge most of the time. Then something like this happens, murder, and all I want to do is climb out of this skin and into my fur so I can run and run and run until all the horror fades."

He placed his large palm over my hand. "Murder doesn't happen often here. It's just bad luck you arrived right around the time Katherine got her comeuppance. If you want to live with humans, Lily, you have to give up some of your Shifter. I learned to manage my impulses. I keep what I hear to myself. I am surrounded by food all day, so I've pretty much grown numb to the scents of humans. Grilled onions have a way of making everything else seem less fouling. On full moons, I go out to the state park where the wildlife is protected, stay away from camping areas, and I let out all my pent- up energy. Winter is especially safe for us because hardly anyone braves the cold to stay in the parks during this time of year."

"Can I go with you next time?"

"If you're still here."

"Right," I agreed. "My truck is in the shop, and the sheriff told me not to leave town. So, as long as I'm a person of interest in this case, I guess I'm stuck here for a bit." And the thought of leaving filled me with trepidation. I couldn't understand why. Much the way I instantly connected with Smooshie, I also felt connected with the town...or at least a few of its inhabitants.

Buzz grabbed a pen and tore a corner off a bill he had on the table. He wrote down a number and handed it to me. "It's my cell phone number. Call me anytime." He tried to smile, but it turned into a grimace.

"Thanks."

CHAPTER 8

I got back to Parker's about five a.m., about the same time a blonde women pulled into his driveway with a carrier holding two coffees and a bag with "Daily Donuts" written on the side.

His girlfriend? The idea bit at me, and I swatted it away.

She knocked on Parker's door as Smooshie dragged me up the walkway toward her. The woman turned, took one look at Smooshie, and grinned.

"Hey, girl," she said. She reached down and scratched the traitorous pit bull behind the ear then looked at me. "Are you new?"

"Sort of. I'm in town visiting."

"Oh, so you're kin to Parker?"

"No. My un—cousin runs The Cat's Meow."

"Oh, Buzz." She smirked. "He's a total flirt, that one. Are you volunteering at the shelter today?" She knocked on the front door again.

Ah. The shelter. I almost forgot that Parker told me he had a slew of volunteers. This woman had to be one of them. I experienced an unsettling amount of relief. "I'm waiting for my truck to get repaired. I've adopted Smooshie here, and Parker was nice enough to let me stay in the loft over his garage."

"Oh." She was smiling, but a little bit of sparkle left her eyes. "I'm Theresa. Theresa Simmons."

"Lily Mason," I obliged.

The door opened. Parker stood in the frame fully dressed in denim and flannel. "Hey, Theresa," he said, grabbing a coffee from the carrier as she ducked past him. He took a sip, his gaze landing on me. "Morning, Lily."

Smooshie barked her own greeting. "I think she wants to run. Did the police shut down the backyard?"

"Yeah." I noted the dark circles under his eyes. I had the strangest urge to offer him comfort, but it wasn't my right. "I'm going to have to cycle the dogs out into the private area where I let the new rescues play until they've been socialized. Sheriff says I won't be able to get out in the main yard for at least the day."

"That bites."

He rubbed his fingers through his hair. "Sure does." He took another sip. "You gonna stand outside all morning or you gonna come on in?"

"I don't want to interrupt your workday." Smooshie nudged me. "Have you gotten any sleep?"

"Not hardly," Parker said. "You?"

"Me either. I walked around town to clear my head."

His eyes widened with alarm. "Someone killed Mrs. Kapersky in my backyard, Lily. Running around in the middle of the night with a murderer on the loose isn't smart."

"Are you calling me dumb?"

"Of course not."

I smiled, letting him off the hook. "It's okay. I spent most of my time with Buzz."

"Your cousin. He's good people."

"He sure is. Thanks again for letting me stay above your garage. I saw his trailer firsthand, and there's barely enough room for one person, let alone a guest." I didn't mention Nadine Booth. "I hope they find Katherine's killer soon."

"Me, too."

"What?" Theresa asked. "Who's been killed?"

"Katherine Kapersky," Parker said. "Someone murdered her inside the shelter's fence last night."

Theresa's hand went to her mouth. "How awful."

"Your dad didn't say anything?"

We all walked into the kitchen. Theresa sat down. "I didn't stop by the house this morning."

I had to ask. "Who's your dad?"

"Sheriff Avery," Parker answered.

"Gotcha." I nodded. "Your mom have him on a diet?"

Theresa gave me an odd look. So did Parker. Crap. I scrunched my nose. "I saw a piece of Kale stuck to his collar. He didn't strike me as the type of guy who would gladly choose to eat something healthy."

Theresa gaped. Closed her mouth. Then laughed. "You got him pegged." She sobered quickly. "Jeesh. I shouldn't be laughing. Not with someone dying and all. What the heck was she doing out there in the middle of the night?"

"Maybe she was dumped," Parker said.

"No." I shook my head. "She was cold, but the snow could have cooled down the body quick."

"You touched her?" Theresa scooted her chair back from me.

"I don't have cooties."

Theresa blushed.

"I had to check for a pulse. It's what anyone would have done."

"I'm not sure I could have done it. It freaks me out just thinking about touching a dead person." She put her left hand on Parker's arm. She wore a wedding band. Made sense, since her last name was Simmons and the sheriff's last name was Avery, but again, it eased something inside me. "I'm sorry something so awful happened last night, Parker. Especially here. But really, that woman."

"She could be difficult."

"Difficult? The devil himself would run away from her."

"I met her for the first time yesterday," I said, "and even I know she was a royal pain in the butt."

Theresa laughed again. "I better get to Rudy's room. He's probably ready to get some exercise."

Parker smiled. "The area should be open. Keith, Larry, and Jason came in early to help me get all the dogs out and back in."

"But not Rudy, right?"

"No, not Rudy. He's all yours." Parker smirked. "I don't know why you don't just adopt him already."

"Jock would never go for it." She heaved a sigh.

"Besides, with Mrs. Kapersky's death, he's going to be up to his eyeballs in council business."

After she had exited the room, I glanced at Parker. "Jock?"

"Jock Simmons. Theresa's husband. He's a lawyer. Has a practice here in town."

"He's on the town council too?"

"Yes. One of five members. Well, four now that... You know."

Smooshie yawned, her tongue curling to the roof of her mouth.

"Why don't you go up and get some sleep? If you're hungry when you wake up, come down for some lunch."

"All right. Thanks."

"I better get to work." He tapped his thigh, and his big silvery-blue beauty immediately moved to his side. "Good boy, Elvis."

"You think Smooshie will ever be that well-behaved?"

Parker laughed. "Probably not."

I said my goodbyes and left Parker's house. As I headed to my apartment, I heard the murmur of a hushed conversation. I recognized Theresa's voice, but the other belonged to a man I'd never heard before.

Katherine Kapersky is dead."

"Shhh," the guy said. "I heard."

"She can't hurt us anymore."

"We have to be careful. If anyone finds out that she was blackmailing you…"

"They won't. I still don't know how she knew."

"You didn't have anything to do with—"

"God, no," Theresa denied. "I…you didn't, did you?"

"Of course not." I could hear the relief in his voice. "We just need to cool things off until this all blows over."

"I love you, Keith."

Ah, one of the volunteers Parker was talking about. So Theresa Simmons was having an affair, and Katherine Kapersky not only knew about it, she was blackmailing her. But for what? Money? Information? Something else?

I remembered Buzz saying she had her hooks into a lot of people. Was this thing, the use of private information for blackmail, what he was referring to? And if the Kapersky woman was blackmailing Theresa Simmons, who else had she backed into a corner? Would someone kill to keep their secrets secret?

Smooshie picked that moment to start yipping excitedly. Theresa and Keith's conversation stopped instantly.

"Smooshie," I said sternly. She ducked as if I would hit her, and I instantly regretted my tone. I knelt in the snow next to her and rubbed my face against hers. "I'm sorry, girl. I would never hurt you." We were far enough away from the couple that I don't believe they knew I overheard them.

The pit bull licked my cheek. I took that as forgiveness, and we went up to the apartment for some much-needed sleep.

I WOKE UP TO THE SOUND OF POLICE SIRENS. SMOOSHIE whined as she jumped from the bed and trotted to the window. She pressed her nose to the pane. I forced myself up to join her. Two sheriffs' vehicles were parked catty-corner to block in Parker's blue dually truck.

Two officers stood out front. One of them was Nadine Booth, one hand on her radio mic and the other on her gun. She looked anxious and miserable.

I hurriedly dressed. "Stay here," I told Smoosh, as if she had any choice in the matter.

The afternoon sun had burned off a lot of the freshly fallen snow from the night before, and the puddles had created slick spots of ice. I carefully avoided the danger zones as I made my way down to Parker's driveway.

Nadine Booth saw me first. "Stay put, Lily."

"What's going on?"

"Official police business. I can't discuss it with you." Though she looked like she'd rather have all the hair tweezed from her head than be in Parker's drive.

"Are you all searching for more evidence out back?"

"No. The sheriff has enough evidence to take a suspect into custody," she said cryptically.

"What's that supposed to mean?"

About that time, Sheriff Avery and another man in uniform came out the front door with Parker. His hands were cuffed behind his back.

"What the hell?"

"Don't get involved, Lily. You have no idea what Parker's capable of, and the evidence supports his arrest."

I ignored Nadine's comment. "Parker!"

He looked at me, his eyes glazed with confusion, shock, and anger. "I didn't do this, Lily."

Without hesitation, I said, "I know."

He nodded once, and his shoulders relaxed. "Call my dad. Tell him I need a lawyer."

Theresa was standing next to me suddenly, her cheeks streaming with tears. "I can't believe they've arrested Parker. There's no way he would've killed anyone—not even Katherine."

"Can you and the volunteers take care of the shelter until this is straightened out?" Parker had told me he had almost twenty dogs, and they would all need attention.

"Of course we can," she said. She dabbed at her cheeks with the back of her hand. A young man a few years her junior joined us on the sidelines.

"It'll be okay, Ther."

Theresa crossed her arms over her chest and huddled in on herself. "I know, Keith."

So this was Keith. He was tall with narrow shoulders and bony hips. He had a scruffy beard like Shaggy from *Scooby Doo*, but his aquamarine eyes and startling dark eyelashes made him attractive. I could see his appeal.

"I have to go to The Rusty Wrench and let Greer know what's going on."

The police cars left the yard in a ceremonial parade. Theresa raised her brow at me. "You've only been in town a day?"

"Yes." I didn't smile. I couldn't. Not with Parker locked up for a crime he didn't commit. I believed that to the bottom of my soul. I debated on whether to take Smooshie or not, but her pounding at the apartment door and her excited yips made the call for me. "Do you have a cell phone number?"

"Yep. Let me write down the number for you." Keith

handed her a wadded up grocery receipt, and Theresa grabbed a pen from her purse. "Call me if you hear anything."

"Definitely," I said. I took the paper from her and shoved it in my pocket. "Thank you."

CHAPTER 9

The Rusty Wrench only had one car out front now, the black SUV. I assumed it was Greer's own vehicle. Smooshie and I waited at the crossing until it was clear then jogged across the street. My boot slipped on a patch of black ice, and I spent a minute windmilling my arms, trying not to fall on my ass. Smooshie's leash caught around my wrist, tugging me forward. She barked, and the sound startled me into gaining my balance.

I unwrapped the leash and then patted her on the head. "Thanks, Smoosh."

She grinned at me, tongue lolling.

"Careful!" I heard Greer shout as he came out of the office door. When I made it to him safely, he said, "The truck's not ready yet. The part won't be in until tomorrow."

I'd run the few blocks to the garage, but I wasn't winded. Endurance was another benefit of being a Shifter. "I'm not here about the truck, sir."

"I work for a living, Miss Mason. Please, call me Greer." He shook his head. "Too many years in the Army. I was a staff sergeant." He said it as if I should know what he was talking about. "What can I do for you?"

"Parker's been arrested," I blurted.

"What?" His rosy complexion paled. "For what? He was doing so much better. I don't understand. What the heck happened?"

Better than what? I wondered. No time to think about that right now. "Katherine Kapersky was murdered."

"Land sakes. Someone finally killed that woman?"

"They think Parker did."

Greer sputtered. "That's ridiculous. My kid may be a lot of things, but cold-blooded murderer ain't one of them."

"He needs a lawyer."

"Jock Simmons, maybe. He does mostly family law, but he's the only one I know. His wife works for Parker."

Ah, Theresa, the cheater. Her marriage to the lawyer didn't matter. The only important thing was to get Parker represented. "Yes, call him. If nothing else, he can recommend a good criminal attorney."

The harsh blare of a car horn rattled my Shifter eardrums. The awful sound was immediately followed by someone shouting obscenities. Then I heard the unmistakable noise of a car crash.

Greer and I turned toward the commotion at the same time. Smooshie yanked on her leash.

My boot slipped on an ice patch, and I went down like I'd been zapped by a witch's fireball. Pain ricocheted up my spine. My pit bull immediately stopped squirming and returned to me, nudging my shoulder.

"I'll live," I told her.

"Christ on a cracker," Greer said. He leaned down and put his arms under my shoulders and hauled me upright. My right butt cheek throbbed.

Now that Smooshie had determined I was okay, she was ready to go check out the car wreck. I noticed that the car was the same black sedan that had nearly run me over the day before. No wonder Smooshie was excited. My girl wanted retribution!

Greer handed me the leash back. "You got this? I'm going to call an ambulance."

"I'll check to see if anyone's hurt." Carefully, Smooshie and I made our way down to the smashed-up car. The driver-side door opened, and a dark-haired woman swung her legs out. I recognized her from the church. She'd been the one who had gone back to talk to the reverend. I'm sure she had a whole slew of driving sins to confess.

The citizen who'd almost become a hood ornament, a stocky older man wearing earmuffs and a wool scarf, started to help her out.

"Wait!" I shouted. "Don't let her get out. She could have a neck or back injury from the impact and moving could aggravate it."

The man raised his hands as if I'd pointed a gun at him. The woman groaned and leaned her shoulder into the backrest of the driver's side seat.

"Are you a nurse?" he asked, frowning.

"Are you?"

"Well, no."

"I'm certified in CPR and first aid," I lied. Technically, I knew enough to get a certification but had never actually taken a course. I'd read a field treatment manual for medics more than a dozen times. Over the years, when my brother Danny had been younger, he'd let me practice some of the techniques, like bandaging wounds, applying tourniquets, stabilizing fractures, and such. I'd gotten pretty good at mummifying him in under sixty seconds.

I knelt in front of the driver. Smooshie sat next to me, sniffing the air. "It'll be okay," I told the woman. "An ambulance is on the way." I detected the scent of formula and talcum powder, suggesting the young woman was a mother. But underneath those pleasant smells was a bitter, sour scent. "Why were you driving so fast?"

She looked at me, her brown eyes clearing as a bit of the shock wore off. "I don't have to answer your questions."

Her defensiveness took me by surprise. I'd give her the benefit of the doubt since she'd just tried to wrap her car around a telephone pole, but I already had a bone to pick with her about trying to run me down the day before.

There was an empty car seat in the back. A box of tissue was stuffed near the console. She had a thirty-two-ounce drink in the cup holder. The plastic container was sweating, so I figured ice was still in it. I looked down at her feet. She wore house slippers. Under the bottom of her long coat, the hem of a nightgown peeked out.

This was not the same put-together woman who'd brushed past me the day before. This was a woman in distress. Why would she go for a drive in her pajamas to get a convenience-store soda?

I met her eyes again, the dark circles under them giving me even more concern. "I'm Lily Mason, and that's Smooshie."

She flicked a glance at the dog and then gave me a wary stare. "Lacy Evans."

"Lacy. Is someone home with your baby?"

The stark guilt in her expression told me what I'd already guessed. "I was only going to be gone five minutes," she said. Tears pooled in the corners of her eyes. "He's sleeping. I'm by myself." She shook her head. "I was only going to be gone five minutes."

She tried to get up, but I stopped her with my hand on her shoulder.

"Let go. I have to get home!"

"You might be injured, Lacy. You're in no condition to go anywhere except the hospital. Is there someone I can call? The baby's father?"

"No!" she answered sharply and immediately. "No father."

"Okay. Is there someone else?"

She nodded. "My mom. Freda Downing. She works at—"

The sirens wailed in the distance, so I knew the ambulance was almost here. "I know who Freda is. She works for my…cousin. I'll call Buzz and tell him to send your mom to your house."

"Thanks." She blinked up at me. I'd seen that look before. I saw in Lacy Evans a scared girl close to falling to pieces. I'd been that girl. Not for the same reasons. Beyond being a single mother, I had no idea what had pushed Lacy to the edge, but I recognized the hopelessness that she wore like a ratty coat.

The police and the ambulance arrived a minute later. I moved out of the way for the EMTs. Lacy got slightly hysterical as the paramedics worked to get her neck in a brace. While they were handling her, I called Buzz, and he sent Freda to her daughter's place, and surprisingly, he asked me to come over and work the lunch shift in her place. I'd waitressed a little back home, so it wasn't a stretch of my talents by any means.

Before leaving the scene, I went to Lacy as they put her on the stretcher and readied her for transport. "Your mom is going to your house. She'll take care of your son. Don't worry, okay?"

She was remarkably calm now as she smiled wanly. I think the paramedic had given her a sedative. She crooked her finger, and I leaned in.

"She's dead, dead, dead," Lacy singsonged. "Krabby Kapersky. She was a terrible person. Did you know she…" Lacy's eyes fluttered closed, and her head lolled sideways.

"What? She what?" I shook her shoulders, but the woman was conked out. "Lacy!"

"We've got to get her in the ambulance, miss. You can meet your friend at the hospital if you'd like."

"She's not my…" The man didn't care. He just wanted to get on his way. "Okay. Thanks."

I wondered exactly what Katherine Kapersky had done to make this young woman glad she was dead. And was it enough to turn the single mom into a killer?

CHAPTER 10

I t was twelve-fifteen when I got to the diner. My uncle had me put Smooshie in his office. He provided me with a pan of water and a large hambone for her and gave me an apron. I felt guilty for locking my new friend into a confined space, but given the amount of chewing and drooling inspired by the hambone, I thought she'd be all right. Still, I worried. "I'm not sure leaving her in here is a good plan."

"She'll be fine," Buzz said.

I gave Smooshie kisses on her bumpy head then left and closed the door behind me. I washed my hands and Buzz gave me a guest check pad and a pencil. "The top copy gets hung up for me. The duplicate with the final amount goes to the customer."

"I've taken an order before."

He cocked his head sideways and gave me a funny

look. "I've been around humans too long. I know you're not a kid, but you still look like one."

I tied the apron around my waist and tucked the pad and pencil in the front pocket. "I forgive you."

He touched his fingers to the left side of his chest. "Thank heavens." He laughed. It was easy and kind, so much like my father's. I swallowed the lump in my throat.

"I'm ready, boss."

He grinned. "Good thing. The place is jumping today. I'm getting people in here I rarely see. Everybody is talking about Katherine Kapersky."

"Murder has a way of bringing people together, I guess."

Opal and Pearl, the two elderly ladies from the day before, sat in the back corner booth, which seemed to be their favorite. The booth nearest the door had five teenagers, two girls and three boys. The one behind them was filled with two women in slacks and dressy tops, not fancy enough for a top-level job, but not casual enough for blue collar. I guessed secretaries or bank tellers because of the toner stains on one of the women's fingers. Besides, they were smiling and laughing. In my experience, people in high-pressure jobs tended to stress no matter where they were. These were women who didn't have to think about work once they left the office.

An older woman with a gentleman who looked to be about Greer's age, somewhere in his fifties, sat in the next booth, and behind them, a mother with three small children. There were two empty booths, three empty tables, and no empty stools at the counter. The place really was hopping.

I started with the first booth of teens.

"What can I get you?"

One of the boys, the all-American type with the perfect hair and perfect nose, said, "I'll have a burger and a side of you, sweetheart."

I might not have the gist of living with humans, but I knew small-town folks. And Shifters or humans, there were the same.

"What's your name?" I asked.

He elbowed his friends, smirking. "James Hanley."

"What would your mama say, James Hanley, if I told her you were disrespecting women?"

He blushed to the roots of his hair. I offered him a look that would melt glass. "You want that burger rare, medium, or well-done?"

"Well-done." He cleared his throat. "Miss."

"Fries on the side?"

"Yes."

"Drink?"

"Coke."

I gave the next boy a don't-mess-with-me-or-I'll-throw-you-in-the-fryer look. "What can I get you?"

"Same," he said.

The third boy said, "Me too." The girls just wanted diet sodas and fries.

On my way back to the kitchen window, I overheard All-American Boy say in a quiet voice, "Tell me you saw her eyes. Dude, that freaked me out."

Oh, crap. My eyes must have partially shifted. Crap. Crap. Crap.

I paused to hear his friends' responses. None of them had seen what he'd seen. I let go of the breath I was holding. Goddess, I had to be more careful.

"Order, Buzz," I said at the window. "Burn three with five frog sticks on the side." I took down five red soda cups from a stack and filled them with ice. I pushed one under regular Coke and the other under the diet fountain. I repeated the step and then finished with the last regular Coke. I loaded a tray and promptly delivered the drinks with a smile. "I'll be back with your order. Holler if you need anything else."

I glanced at the still red-faced boy who'd seen my accidental shift. I didn't know who he was more scared of—

his mother or me. He looked away quickly. I had a feeling he wouldn't be asking me for much.

I followed the process all the way down the line of customers, seating a few new tables as they came in. Buzz peeked his head out once and said, "Looks like you got it under control."

I smiled. He didn't say it, but I knew he was impressed, and for some reason, his approval made me happy.

Tom Jones came in around one o'clock with a blonde on his arm. I recognized Bridgette, the soloist from the choir. She clung to the orthodontist's arm like Scotch tape. When he saw me, he frowned. "You work here?"

I grabbed two laminated menus. "I'm just helping out my cousin today. His waitress had a family emergency."

"Oh, that's nice of you."

"I'm Bridgette Jones," the woman said, eyeballing me from head to toe. "Tommy's wife."

Aww, the wife. "I'm Lily," I said. "Nice to meet you."

Tom didn't elaborate on how we'd met, so I didn't mention it either. Bridgette had been part of the choir that Katherine Kapersky led. Surely, Tom had told her about the murder. Maybe she was a fragile type?

"Booth or table? I have one of each left."

Tom looked down at the blonde. She said, "Booth."

"Right this way." I seated them in the booth next to Opal and Pearl, who happily chatted about how badly maintained the roads were in town. Pearl said she'd seen two trucks slide around as they went down the street. After witnessing Lacy's wreck, I agreed with their concerns.

"Thank you," Bridgette said. "I want a sweet iced tea and a garden salad."

I jotted down her order. "You got it. What can I get for you, Tom?"

He swallowed hard like a bug had hit the back off his throat. "Uhm, I'll take a cheeseburger with the works, coffee, and an ice water."

"Side of fries?"

"Yep."

I wanted to ask him if he knew more about the case, but he acted like he didn't want me talking to him in front of his wife. Plus, he'd been so hostile about Parker's guilt, I wasn't sure I wanted to discuss the case with him.

The in and out of customers slowed down shortly after one, but the place was still packed. Stools squeaked, catsup glurped, silverware clinked, and people chatted. Most of the gossip was about Katherine Kapersky's murder.

With all the stations taken care of, I sat at an empty table and rolled silverware, stuffed napkin holders, and topped off empty salt and pepper shakers…and listened.

"I can't believe the old bitty is dead."

"Never met anyone who had it coming more."

"Do you really think it was murder? Couldn't it have been an accident?"

"Are you going to ask Carmen to the winter formal?" Teenagers. They lived in such small, pristine bubbles. I couldn't imagine a time when all I had to worry about was being asked to a high school dance.

"I heard Parker Knowles, that guy who has all those dogs, did it."

"My neighbor John said the sheriff hauled him away in cuffs."

"Have you seen Parker Knowles? I've had fantasies about him and handcuffs, but they have nothing to do with murder."

I tensed. This conversation was going on between the two ladies in slacks. Their giggles made me want to sharpen my claws on their faces.

"What did you tell the sheriff?" My ears perked up, and being a werecougar, that was a literal thing. Bridgette Jones had asked the question, and I waited to hear her husband's answer.

"The death was suspicious. They turned Katherine's

body over to the state medical examiner this morning. There's nothing more I can do."

"What about Parker?"

"He looks guilty as hell." Tom's tone softened. "I don't want you to worry about anything, Bridge."

"Is he going to jail?"

"Probably. The evidence against him is stacked high."

I white-knuckled a salt shaker. The thought of Parker going to prison and not running the rescue center raised bile in my throat. Those pitties needed his protection. In my heart, I knew the sheriff had arrested the wrong guy. Right now, I felt like the only person who believed in his innocence.

As unobtrusively as possible, I turned in my seat until I could get a better view of the couple.

Bridgette sighed. "What about Ed? He knows something. I should tell the sheriff I saw him fighting with her."

"Let it go, Bridgette. It's best if you stay out of this all together."

A sibling spat might have led to a violent confrontation. Would Tom let the sheriff know about the altercation? Even if Ed had nothing to do with her death, he might have been the last one to see her before someone crushed in her skull. He might even be able to clear Parker's name.

Bridgette pulled a mirror from her purse and fixed her lip gloss. "I hope the choral isn't canceled."

"Don't be surprised if it is, sweetheart. Katherine's death will change things around here."

"You've got to be kidding me!" I heard Buzz yell from the back.

A loud *rrrr-rrrr-RRR* followed by a playful *ruff!* had me scooting out of the booth and hurrying to his office.

Buzz stood in the doorway, his expression incredulous as he stared inside. I poked my head around his torso. The landline phone was on the floor, the receiver part chewed clean off, a roll of paper towels had been unrolled and shredded into large flakes of confetti, and a stale cup of coffee had knocked over onto the computer keyboard. Right in front of the door, just past the empty bowl of water and the gnawed-on hambone was a steaming pile of poop with a yellow puddle of pee next to it.

Sweet Goddess. My pittie had destroyed Buzz's office, and there she was, sitting in the middle of the chaos, her ears twitching, her tongue lolling out of her smile as her tail swished the debris back and forth. When I named her Smooshie, I had no idea she'd live up to it in such a faithful way. She'd just about smooshed everything in sight.

"She's a damn wrecking ball, Lily."

"I'm sorry, Buzz. I'll get it cleaned up. But for the

record, I told you it wasn't a good idea to leave her in here alone."

"Noted," Buzz said. His head dropped. "It's gonna smell like doggie butt in there for a week."

IT TOOK ME FIFTEEN MINUTES TO CLEAN UP SMOOSHIE'S mess. I couldn't be mad at her. If someone locked me in a room for an hour with nothing but a bone to keep me busy, I'd probably find ways to amuse myself as well. I took her out back to see if she needed to go again, and by the time I got inside, Freda had returned.

"Everything okay?" I asked.

Her smile was thin and tired. "Lacy's back home with Paulie. He's such a sweet angel. He was still sound asleep by the time I got there."

"Is Lacy going to be okay?"

"I hope so. Unfortunately, Lacy's accident and the fact Paulie was left alone got the attention of Lacy's social worker. Damn Katherine. She's the one who sicced the social services on my daughter, all because she's a single mother. That woman didn't know how to mind her own business." Freda huffed, obviously upset about the entire situation. "Thank you for calling me. Because of you, I was able to get to her house before the police arrived. It's the only thing that kept them from taking

Paulie. Lacy's a good mom. She loves that boy, you know."

I was eighteen when I had to take on the responsibility of my seven-year-old brother on my own. I understood the desire to escape at times. And once, I'd gone to the store while he was sleeping, but he'd been nine-years-old, not nine-months-old.

I didn't want to judge Lacy, but between her reckless driving and leaving her baby at home alone, I truly believed she needed help. The professional kind. And she also moved up on my suspect list. Lacy knew something about Katherine Kaspersky's death—either that, or she was the one who'd bashed in the woman's head.

"I hope everything works out," I told her. I touched her arm and tried to convey my compassion.

Freda nodded. "Thanks for covering for me, Lily."

"You bet."

After I went over the orders in process and passed her the apron, I went to the kitchen to say goodbye to Buzz.

"You did great. Thanks again."

"No problem. It was fun." I really wanted to check out Ed. Could Katherine Kapersky's brother have killed her? There were times when my brother drove me nuts, but never to the point where I'd want to hurt him. "Do you know where I could find Ed Miles?"

"Why do you want to find Katie's brother?"

"I just want to ask him a few questions."

"You should stay out of this, Lils. No good can come from getting involved in human affairs. Just let the sheriff handle it."

"The sheriff has tunnel vision," I told him. "He's made up his mind about Parker, which means he's not looking for the real killer."

He looked at me, brows raised. "You're just like your mother. She had the same drive to find the truth. And she was as stubborn as all get-out."

The idea I shared those qualities with my mother pleased me to no end. Buzz probably hadn't known that Mom had a magical talent for sussing out lies—another gift she'd passed on to me.

"I still think this is a bad idea, Lily. What do you know about investigating?"

"My best friend Haze Kinsey is the Chief of Police in Paradise Falls now. She used to be FBI, and I have been integral in helping her solve more than one or two crimes." I didn't add that it had been three crimes total. An expert, I wasn't, but I also wasn't about to let the sheriff's department railroad Parker for a crime he didn't commit.

My uncle sighed heavily and shook his head. "I can see you aren't going to let this go. I caution you to move forward with care, Lily."

"That's how I roll."

A smile flickered. "I don't know where Ed lives. He comes in for lunch most days, but I haven't seen him today." My expression must have reflected my disappointment because Buzz added, "However, there are two things that Ed really loves." He held up a finger. "Fly Fishing." He held up another finger. "Drinking."

I smirked. "It's too cold for fly fishing."

"Exactly," Buzz said. "I sometimes see him at Nix's Bar on Oak Street. I'd hazard to guess you might find him there tonight."

I went up on my tiptoes and kissed Buzz on the cheek. A move that surprised both of us. He touched the spot where my lips had landed. "Go on," he said, his voice soft. "And take Armageddon with you."

Smooshie was tied up near the back door now, lying down with her chin on her paws. I'd never seen such a pitiful, sad face. When I reached her, I gave her neck a scratch, and she perked right up. "You're a good girl, Smooshie, don't let anyone tell you different."

It was not quite two o'clock yet. I decided to go back to the shelter and check in. I wanted to talk to Theresa. If Katherine had been blackmailing her, then she had reason to want the woman dead, too.

CHAPTER 11

"**T**hanks for bringing coffee and pie. Buzz's apple is one of my favorites." Theresa Simmons took another bite. "How did you know?"

"I'm psychic," I told her.

She stopped chewing, her eyes wide.

I laughed. "I asked Buzz what you liked."

"Oh." She giggled. "That makes more sense."

I'd brought the apple pie with me from The Cat's Meow. I was hoping the pastry bribe might get her to open up. I found it hard to believe that Theresa would do anything to hurt Parker. But there was only one way to find out. Activate my witchy powers and see if Theresa lied to me.

Keith walked into the kitchen with Smooshie following

close behind him. She skittered over to me and rubbed her side against my leg, her backside wagging as she licked my hand. "Someone missed you," he said.

Fifteen minutes in dog time feels like fifteen years. "Thanks for taking her out for me." I'd hoped Theresa and I would get more time to speak alone, but it didn't seem like it was going to happen.

So it surprised me when she turned to him and said, "Could you take Elvis out? He's looking pretty blue."

I smiled at her description since he was a silver-blue in color. However, he did look depressed. I'd only spent one day with Parker, but I knew how much he relied on Elvis for comfort and stress relief. I imagined he was crawling out of his skin down at the sheriff's station.

Keith wiggled his nose, red from the cold, but nodded. "Okay."

After he had left, Theresa leaned forward, her elbows on the table. She cupped her hands around the warm to-go cup of coffee. She glanced at the table, up to me, over to the sink, then back to me. "I didn't mean to fall in love with Keith," she said.

I nearly choked on my own bite of pie. "Of course not."

"Jock and I have been married for twelve years. It used to be real good between us."

Her sudden confession caught me off-guard. I guess my

witchy juju worked fast on humans. I offered her a smile and nodded in encouragement.

"The past four or five years, it's been like living with a stranger." Her voice caught. "We don't talk anymore. We stopped making love a long time ago." She shivered and took a sip of coffee.

"He's a lawyer, right?"

"A really good one. It's all he ever wanted to be." She met my gaze with a certain amount of pride as she said, "He had a football scholarship out of high school, but when his grades started slipping, he quit playing college ball because becoming a lawyer was more important to him than sports. He always had his eye out for his future."

"What happened? Between the two of you, I mean?"

"Public service, I suppose. Jock used to be home at six every night without fail, but seven years ago he ran for a seat on the town council and won. He was voted president his second year, and he started spending evenings in meetings at the courthouse or at events, charity and business stuff. I tried to be supportive, I really did."

"He was the president?"

"Yes, for two years. Then Katherine Kapersky…" her mouth pursed sourly as she said the dead woman's name, "…was elected president. Jock didn't take it well. I think his anger made it harder for me to reach him. I ended up getting the brunt of it whenever he was home. After a while, we were two ships passing in the night." She looked down at the table. "I'm terrible, aren't I? A woman was murdered, and here I am making excuses for cheating on my husband."

"It sounds like you're in an untenable situation," I said sympathetically. I waited a beat. "Did Katherine know about the affair?"

"What? How…?" Her shoulders slumped. "Yes." She turned her knees out and looked toward the front door as if plotting an escape. "She was such an awful person. I shouldn't be glad she's dead, but I am."

"She obviously didn't need money," I said. "What did she want from you in return for keeping your secret?"

"I work for Parker four days a week, but I also do billing for the hospital. Katherine wanted to know certain things about a few people."

"Which people?"

Keith opened the door and led Elvis into the room. The poor dog trudged to his doggie bed and curled up, releasing a sigh of sadness that hit me right in the feels.

Theresa stood up so suddenly she rocked the table. She glanced at me warily. What did she expect me to do? Yell, "Freeze!" and make a citizen's arrest for adultery? "I better go make my rounds," she said. "Let me know if you hear anything from Parker."

After Theresa had gone into the shelter, Keith lingered

for a minute. "I can't believe Parker killed Mrs. Kapersky."

"I don't think he did," I said defensively.

Keith blinked. "I guess that came out wrong. I don't, either. I've known the guy for a couple of years. Never met anyone more patient."

"Why do you think someone would frame Parker?"

"The only person I'd accuse of that is Katherine, but I doubt she intended to get murdered, much less throw the blame at Parker."

"About half the town seems to have a motive. Katherine wasn't very well-liked."

"Not liking someone isn't a good reason to kill them." Keith seemed truly nonplussed by the idea of murder.

"Some people don't need a good reason to kill," I said, thinking of the way my family had been murdered.

Keith nodded, still looking confused, but in an adorable way. I could see why Theresa was attracted to him. I sensed his kindness and his loyalty. He was a gentle man, and I marked him—and Theresa—off my suspect list.

I'D CALLED FOR A CAB, WHICH IT TURNED OUT THERE WERE three in Moonrise. Not three companies. Three cabs. All of them were busy at the moment, so it was nearly five when the one I'd booked finally arrived.

I'd walked Smooshie, and she'd dropped a huge load and peed like she wouldn't be happy unless all the snow was yellow.

"Please don't lick, eat, scratch, or otherwise smoosh anything, okay?"

She agreed by swiping her tongue across my cheek.

I left her in the apartment with the television on for company, because I was pretty sure she wouldn't be allowed inside the sheriff's station. I hadn't heard from Parker, and Greer wasn't answering his phone. So, I was going to go find out for myself exactly what was going on.

The Carlton County Sheriff's Department was attached to the Carlton County Jail out on a gravel road just outside of town. It was in a large clearing by itself. No trees or buildings for miles around. The jail had a tall fenced-in area out front, where several men sat at a picnic table. They wore coats with orange reflector strips over orange jumpers and sandals with heavy socks on.

I got out of the cab. "Will you wait for me?" I asked the driver.

"For how long?" The driver, a rumpled man with a day-old beard and too much aftershave, eyeballed me like I was a felon.

"I'm not sure."

"Fine. The meter's running."

"Okay," I agreed. "Just don't leave." I did not want to get stuck out in the middle of nowhere without a ride home.

As I hurried up the sidewalk, I pulled my coat tightly around me. I felt the hard gazes of the prisoners on me, but I kept going, head down.

Until I smelled sweet mint.

I glanced at the yard. At a table by himself, his jacket collar up, Parker sat with his head in his hands.

"Hey," I said. "Parker!"

He looked up at me, his eyes wild. He wore a mixture of fear and anxiety, an energy I was startled to see on him. Worse, he didn't seem to recognize me.

"It's Lily," I said. "Remember, Smooshie's Lily?"

He blinked.

Another inmate, a bald man, thick with a beer gut, shouted, "I've got your smooshie right here, darlin'," as he grabbed his crotch and thrust his pelvis at me.

Parker jumped up from his seat and catapulted himself at the guy as an angry roar of rage ripped from him. A guard was on him before he could make contact and held him back.

"That's it, Knowles!" Another guard swooped in for the assist as I watched helplessly while they dragged him inside the building.

I hadn't thought Parker was capable of murder, but now I wasn't sure. His violent reaction to the other prisoner made me realize I didn't know him at all. Had I let my hormones override my good sense? Did the police have it right?

I shook my head. While I had to admit Parker might be capable of murder, I still believed he wasn't stupid enough to leave a body in his backyard. Besides, I'd been there when he first saw Katherine in the field. I hadn't sensed any deception in his reaction. He'd been genuinely surprised and distressed.

The inmate who'd grabbed his crotch and thrust at me started laughing. A bubbling anger surfaced inside me, and I could feel my claws coming out. Literally. If there hadn't been two fourteen-foot fences topped with razor wire between me and the jerk, I'd have jumped over and tore him up.

Once again, I had to remind myself that this wasn't Paradise Falls. I was in a town of humans, and I had to blend in. Besides, I couldn't help Parker if I got myself imprisoned, too. I squeezed my fingers into fists, the cougar claws biting into my skin as I pulled myself together.

I didn't know if they would let me see Parker. Especially now that he'd been hauled off for nearly attacking someone, but I was determined to try. Inside the front door of the sheriff's department was a gray-walled room with a gray linoleum floor. On the left was a glass window that showed another gray room. It had three booths with monitor and phones. The door said, "Inmate Visitors." Below that was a sign that said, "Visiting hours between 8:00 a.m. and 5:00 p.m."

Shoot. It was 5:45 p.m.

On the right side of the lobby, behind another window, was a young man in uniform. He was typing something into the computer and had barely glanced at me since I'd walked in. At the bottom of his window was an opening meant for exchanging paperwork and such. As I waited for the officer to finish what he was doing, I continued looking around the depressing lobby. I noted another door to my right. It was made from thick metal and had no handle. I figured it was a secured entrance into the prison.

On the wall between the visitors' room and the please-be-ignored-here check-in, I saw a corkboard with CCW (Carry Concealed Weapons) information, instructor cards, a most-wanted bulletin, and a flyer for the charity choral event taking place at Reverend Kapersky's church this Sunday. I wondered if Katherine's murder merited the cancellation of the event. After all, the rev had a funeral to plan.

The young uniformed officer tapped on his side of the window. "Hey, lady. What do you need?"

He looked bored and irritated. I didn't know if it was because his job sucked or because he didn't want to deal with me. "I'd like to see Parker Knowles, please."

"Prisoners are only allowed visitors between the hours of eight a.m. and five p.m. Didn't you see the sign?"

"Well, is that a hard-and-fast rule?"

"You know this is a prison, right? It's where we keep people who break the law." He crossed his arms, his expression dour. "We enforce the rules. *All* of them."

"I'll come back tomorrow," I said.

"Good call. I'm really not in the mood to arrest you." With a final look of censure, he sat down and started typing again.

I heard a buzz and a loud metallic click. Nadine Booth walked out the secured door and looked curiously startled to see me. The door swung shut behind her with a final, deep thud.

"Lily? What are you doing here?"

"I wanted to check on Parker."

"He's okay," she said.

"I saw what happened in the yard. Where was he taken?"

"To isolation. It's really the best thing for him. He's real anxious and jumpy."

"Wouldn't you be?" Worry jabbed at me. "This is ridiculous. He didn't kill Katherine."

"No offense, Lily, but you've only been in town two days. You don't really know Parker or what he's capable of."

"So what? It doesn't mean I'm wrong about his innocence."

"We follow the evidence." Her gaze showed doubt, though. "C'mon. I'll walk you out."

She escorted me out of the lobby and into the cold winter afternoon.

I pointed to the fenced-in area. "Why are all those guys wearing sandals in the dead of winter?"

Nadine chuckled. "Sandals make it hard to run away."

"Oh." The practicality behind the reason surprised me. People didn't always go for the simplest solution, and sandals were pretty freaking simple. "That makes sense. Really, it's the only thing that has made sense since they arrested Parker."

Nadine looked tired. She put her hand on my forearm. For a moment, she held on to my arm, and I could see some internal debate going on in her head as she hemmed and hawed. Finally, she said, "They found blood on Parker's baseball bat. And his fingerprints were on the handle."

"Oh, crap." Fingerprints on the murder weapon were strong evidence.

I needed to get busy finding the real killer before Parker ended up convicted of capital murder. And I got the sense that Nadine might just help me. "You free tonight?"

Nadine cocked her head. "Maybe. What you got in mind?"

"Drinks at Nix's Bar are in order after this dreadful day."

"You know," she said, her shoulders slumped. "I'd really like that."

"Great. You want to meet there about seven?"

"See you there."

I returned to the cab, eager for the evening. Tonight I would observe Ed Miles to see if he was a viable suspect, and pick Nadine's brain for more information on the case against Parker. Plus, I really could use a drink. It was a win, win, win.

CHAPTER 12

"This is a bunch of horse hockey," Greer Knowles said. "It ain't fair, them holdin' my boy." The older man ran his hand through his hair, reminding me so much of his son. "The judge won't arraign him until tomorrow." He rubbed his eyes. "Parker doesn't do well in confined spaces. Not since the war. He needs to breathe." His pinched expression worried me.

"He'll be okay, won't he? At least for a little while?"

Elvis whined as if he knew we were talking about his person. I leaned down and stroked the dog's soft fur. Elvis turned his big, sad eyes on me before sighing deeply and sinking into his dog bed. I wished there was a way I could help him feel better, but I knew the only way to do that was to get Parker out of jail. "Don't worry, Elvis. Parker will be back soon."

Smooshie tucked her cold nose into my armpit.

"She sure has taken to you."

"The feeling is mutual." As I scratched behind Smooshie's floppy ears, I wondered what in the world I ever did before her. I'd never had a companion like her, certainly not in a Shifter town, where having pets was a no-no. Aside from finding the idea of "owning" an animal abhorrent, there was also the danger of Shifters attacking the weaker species. Sometimes the primal urges overcame intellect and empathy. "Are you sure you're okay to stay here tonight, Greer? You don't mind taking care of the dogs? Including Smooshie?"

"Nah." He shook his head. "I help Parker every once in a blue moon if he needs me. I don't mind a bit. Besides, I'll have help until ten, and then it will just be a matter of letting them out to toilet when they need it."

Theresa, Keith, and Larry had gone home for the day, but a second set of volunteers had arrived soon after.

"Greer, I want to ask you something, but I don't want you to get the wrong idea."

"Let me have it."

"Does Parker have a reason for wanting Katherine Kapersky dead?"

The tips of the older man's ears turned a burgundy red, and the grim line of his mouth said I might have hit a little too close to home.

I put my hand on his. Even his knuckles had calluses. "I want to help clear Parker's name."

The deep lines around his eyes eased. "It's nice to know he has someone in his corner."

Smooshie chose that moment to lick my armpit. I jerked back. "Ew. Smoosh." I laughed as she went back for a second go. "No licking the pits. Yuck." I'd put on the only nice dress I had for my night out with Nadine, and unfortunately, it was sleeveless.

Greer smiled. "You're a good person, Lily. I can tell." He got up for a glass of water. When he sat back down, he said, "Well, you probably heard that Katherine was doing everything in her power to get Parker's shelter kicked out of town. But the truth is, Katherine took out her frustrations on Parker because she was mad at me."

"Did you overcharge her on a tune-up?"

He looked offended, and I patted his hand. "I'm kidding."

A smile ghosted on his lips. "I saw her for a little while."

"Saw her?"

He raised a brow.

"Oh. *Saw* her." I grimaced. "How long did y'all date?"

"It was about seven years ago before the rev moved to town. We were only together for a couple of months. I broke it off, and she hated me for breaking her heart." He shook his head. "She wasn't always mean-spirited."

It was difficult to imagine that Katherine had ever been nice. "Then why did you break up?"

"I didn't love Katie. I couldn't. Once you've met and married the love of your life, everything else pales in comparison. It's hard to compete with the dead. Katie never forgave me for still being in love with my wife."

I'd almost forgotten that Greer was a widow. "Parker told me his mom died when he was in high school."

"It was tough for him."

"For both of you," I said. "Thanks for talking to me."

"You're easy to talk to, Lily." He smiled. "I think my son would agree with me."

My chest squeezed. A knock at the door spared me from a reply. "I think that's my ride." I stood up and brushed dog hair off my midnight-blue dress. Well, as much as I could. "I won't stay out too late."

"You go on now." He shooed me. "Smooshie, Elvis, and I have an evening of John Wayne and popcorn planned."

I grabbed my coat from the hall rack. "You rock." I couldn't help but feel unsettled, though. The victim had been found in Parker's backyard. The weapon had been on his back porch. And to make matters worse, he had a motive. Trying to prove Parker's innocence was becoming less a challenge and more than impossible. My doubts made me miss my BFF even more. So I asked myself, WWHD? What would Hazel do?

She'd cast a spell to locate evidence or a lead in the case, but since my vaguely witchy powers seemed to only include being a lie detector, I'd have to rely on non-magical options for the time being.

Pool balls clattering, glasses clinking, and country music blaring from the jukebox marked Nix's Bar as a jumpin' joint. The place was standing-room only as I made my way inside. The men mostly wore Wrangler jeans, button-down western shirts—the kind with snaps. The women wore high-waisted snug-fitting jeans with body-hugging T-shirts and western shirts, their pants tucked into fancy cowboy boots.

Suddenly, I didn't want to take my coat off.

"Lily!" I barely heard my name over the racket. My Shifter ears were suffering hardcore. How could humans bear listening to all of this noisy confusion? Nadine, dressed in jeans and a pink T-shirt that complemented her dark-brown hair, was sitting at a tall two-person table back in the corner. She waved her hand at me then beckoned me over to an empty stool next to her.

"This place is hoppin' for a Monday."

"This place is busy every night. They have pool leagues through the week that play here."

There were six pool tables, all of them with games going.

"I can't believe you got an open seat," I said with genuine respect. "I'm surprised someone didn't try to take it."

She smirked and flexed her fist. "Oh. They tried."

I laughed and pushed myself up onto the chair. Nadine circled her finger in the air. A waitress came over for our drink order.

"Two beers," she said to our server then looked at me. "Is that okay?"

It had been a long and crazy two days. "Two beers and two whiskey chasers," I said, upping the ante on our night out.

Nadine hooted. "Blammo!" She clapped me on the shoulder. "I'm in!"

A few beers and a few shots wouldn't get me drunk, but it would be more than plenty to loosen Nadine up enough to maybe share some information about Parker's arrest. I didn't know what she could tell me that would make a difference to my investigation, but if there was even a chance something might help Parker, I had to try.

I spotted Ed Miles at the bar. He was dressed just about

the same as he had been when I'd seen him in the diner, right down to the string tie. He nursed a cocktail in a highball glass. By the looks of it, it could've been an Old Fashioned. I flared my nostrils. The smell of beer, booze, cheap body spray and sweat crawled into my nose. Gross. This many humans crammed together threatened to overwhelm my super-charged senses.

"You all right?" Nadine asked.

"Sure," I told her. "Just getting my bearings. New town, new faces."

"Finding a dead body doesn't help," she said.

I glanced up at her. "No, that kind of sucked."

"So, how long you staying in town?"

"I haven't decided." I knew Buzz didn't want me to stay, but I wasn't sure I wanted to leave. At least not right away. "I'm in between homes at the moment."

"Is that why you tracked down Buzz?"

I had the distinct feeling I was on the wrong side of this interrogation. I wanted answers from Nadine. It seemed as if she wanted the same from me. "All my family have passed on. Until recently, I thought I had no other kin. Then I found out about Buzz."

"Wow. This was like a real live Oprah moment then, huh? Meeting your long-lost cousin."

"Something like that."

Nadine flipped her hair back over her shoulder. "He likes having you around."

I met her gaze. "Really?"

"Yeah," Nadine answered. "Really. I can tell."

Which meant he hadn't actually said so. I knew Buzz and Nadine had a thing together, but I doubted my uncle confided in anyone. He'd made it clear that he stayed out of human business. "Do they know what time Katherine actually died?"

The abrupt change of conversation startled Nadine. I was working on the assumption this would be a little *quid pro quo*. I answered her question, now she could answer mine. And she did. "The medical examiner said she died between nine and eleven p.m. of strangulation."

"Not a traumatic head wound?" This was a new twist in an already twisted murder. Someone strangled Katherine and then smashed her head in with a bat? "Did—"

Nadine held up her hand. "My turn. Do you know if Buzz has ever been married?"

I was pretty sure he'd never mated, but married was another story. "I don't think so, but I don't know for certain."

"Crap."

I shook my head and smiled. "Do the police really

believe Parker strangled Katherine then hit her with his bat? Couldn't someone have planted her blood on the thing?"

"You really think he was framed, don't you?"

I gave her an assessing look. "Don't you? I don't know you well, Nadine, but I believe you're a smart cookie. I don't think my *uh*—cousin would see someone who didn't have a good head on her shoulders. Doesn't this all seem too tidy? I found the body in Parker's back-yard. He picked up the bat when he came out to check for an intruder. And I can vouch without a shadow of a doubt that he was startled to see a dead woman. He did not kill Katherine Kapersky, and whoever did is banking on lazy police work to point the finger away from them and toward Parker."

"But why would they set up Parker?"

"Two birds, one stone. Either Parker was targeted for the fall because someone hated him as much as they hated Katherine. Or maybe it was just a matter of convenience."

"There were no drag marks out to her body. The only footprints belong to a size eleven men's shoe matching Parker's snow boots, and a size six women's boot matching your size. Well, and a bunch of dog prints were everywhere, but other than that, nothing. Nada. You tell me how a killer walked out over a blanket of snow with the victim, bashed her in the head, and got clean away without leaving any evidence behind."

She drank the whiskey shot when the waitress delivered our drinks. I followed suit and put up two fingers for two more before the gal could leave.

"Oh," Nadine added. "And Parker's fingerprints were the only fingerprints we found on the bat."

"That can't be," I said.

"It's true." She took a sip of beer. "We tested ten ways to Sunday for any latent prints, and we only found Parker's."

"But he showed me the bat earlier when we'd had dinner."

"Yeah, so?"

"So, I touched it. I held it and even gave it a little swing." When she gave me a blank stare, I added, "Somebody wiped down that bat. Why would Parker wipe it down *before* he killed someone? He wouldn't. A killer wipes down a weapon after the crime is committed. And as to his boots, he keeps them on the back porch with the bat. How hard would it be for someone to put them on and carry the body out into the yard?"

"Jesus, Lily. You are killing my buzz." She giggled, so I knew I wasn't killing it too badly. "But you're right. A killer would wipe down after the crime. So, if someone used Parker's bat and wiped it down…"

"He picked it up when he came out after I discovered the body."

"I hate to say this, but I think you're making a whole lot of sense."

"You'll get used to it," I said.

She gave me a sideways look then chuckled. "I hope when this is all over you decide to stick around. I think we could be friends."

I clinked my beer glass against hers. "I think we already are."

"So, any other observations you want to impart?"

"I overheard Bridgette Jones…"

"I think of the Renee Zellweger movies every time I hear her name."

We have a theater back at Paradise Falls, because even Shifters and witches like to be entertained, so I knew whom she was talking about. "I prefer the books," I said.

"You don't get to see Colin Firth in a book," she countered.

"True. Anyhow, I overheard Bridgette say she saw Ed arguing with Katherine."

Nadine shook her head. "Most people aren't so forth-coming about being a snoop."

"I don't have time to be coy. You know Parker won't do well in jail."

"Everyone knows," she admitted quietly, "even the Sheriff, but he's being a jerk about accommodations. Look, Katherine and Ed fighting isn't exactly news. Those two never really got along."

I motioned to where he sat at the bar. "I saw them have a minor standoff at the diner yesterday afternoon. Something about him not being in church."

"Wait," Nadine said, suddenly sober. "The sheriff questioned him today. He said he hadn't seen her since yesterday at lunch."

"Why would he lie?"

"Maybe he killed her." Nadine shrugged. "But I find it hard to believe. Ed's personality is the exact opposite of his sister's. Plus, he's knackered most of the time."

"Why would—"

She lifted her hand and cut me off. "Officially, I can't let you question a person of interest, Lily." She stood up. "But unofficially, we are two women painting the town, and there is no harm in chatting a fellow up at the bar."

I stood up, unzipped my coat, and laid it over the stool.

"Wowzers," Nadine said. "Pretty smokin'. Ed will be too stupefied to know he's being interrogated."

More than one man gawked at me. I wasn't so much flattered as extremely uncomfortable. "I didn't know what to wear," I protested.

"You look great," she said. "If I were your size, I'd prob-ably just wear a bikini and a belly ring."

"That wouldn't keep me very warm."

She looked around at all the dudes. "There are many ways to stay warm, my friend." She clapped me on the back again. "Let's go see a man about an alibi."

CHAPTER 13

A lot of eyes were on me, from men and women alike, as Nadine and I navigated the crowded room to the bar. I seriously regretted not going a more casual clothing route. A buxom woman with broad shoulders nudged me hard as I passed by her. I stopped and met her glare with a smile.

"I'm sorry," I said. "I didn't mean to bump you." The woman scowled, so I added, "That's a real pretty shirt." She wore a pink V-neck that accentuated her curves. "I wish I had the body to pull it off."

For a moment, she appeared befuddled as she assessed my sincerity. Finally, she grunted. "Thanks."

Nadine, who'd been ready for a fight, leaned in close to my ear. "You handle yourself very well, Lily. Lynnie Collins likes to fight. I've never seen her so thoroughly unarmed."

"I worked as a cocktail waitress for a couple of years."

Back in 2005. "I learned early on in the job that taking a stranger's anger personally just makes things worse." I shrugged. "Besides, it *is* an attractive blouse." I looked at Nadine. "With your coloring and curves, it would look totally hot on you."

"I can see your cousin doesn't have the market cornered on charm."

"I don't think that kind of thing is genetic."

"Says you."

I scanned the room as we headed toward the bar. It was mostly habit. When you grow up in a Shifter community, you make sure you know where any problems might be coming from. Especially when drinking is involved.

A tinkle of laughter reminded me of my witch friend's familiar, making me a little homesick. Two honey-blonde women and a dark brunette were sitting behind one of the pool tables, ogling a particularly firm butt in jeans, and giggling like school girls.

The brunette was Lacy Evans.

My chest squeezed when I recognized her. What was she doing in here after having a major car accident—and getting into trouble with social services? I hoped Freda was at least babysitting her grandson.

Nadine rubbed her shoulder against mine. "Nice stick, eh?"

"Huh?"

"The guy at the pool table with the cutie-patootie."

I managed to move my gaze to take in the rest of him. He had dark-brown hair. It was a little longer on top and had a healthy shine. His face could have fit right in with da Vinci's golden ratio for the perfect face. Add in his piercing emerald-green eyes, and I could see why all the girls were gaga for him.

"He's all right," I said noncommittally.

Nadine nearly choked on her drink. "Yeah, right. Saying Ryan Petry is all right is like saying the Sistine Chapel is a nice little painting."

The name rang a bell. Where had I heard it before? "Ryan Petry?"

"Most just call him Doc Ryan. He grew up around here, went off to college and became a veterinarian, then came back and opened a practice."

"Oh, he's the vet." I remembered Parker talking about him. They were friends, he'd said. *Parker.* What he must be going through in jail made my heart hurt. "Parker told me about him."

"You got it bad for that guy."

She didn't have to specify Parker for me to know whom she meant. "I barely know him," I protested.

"Dang, girl. He's a nice guy, but he's got his own issues, you know."

"Don't we all."

"That's about a fact." She laughed.

About that time, a middle-aged man in tight jeans and a black shirt strolled over to us.

"Uh-oh," Nadine said under her breath.

"Nadine," the guy said, his caramel-colored eyes warmed as he glanced from her to me. "You going to introduce me to your friend?"

"I wouldn't introduce you to my enemy, much less my friend."

The guy laughed as if she was joking, but I could tell by her tone she wasn't. He held his hand out to me. Reluctantly, mostly because of Nadine's reaction to him, I shook his hand.

"I'm Jock Simmons," he said. "I haven't seen you around before."

His muscles were bulky. The kind of build you get from working out with weights. His hair was neatly slicked with product. Something that smelled faintly citrusy, like bergamot.

"Oh," I told him, taking my hand back before he plopped down a flag and claimed my palm as territory. "I know your wife. Theresa, right?"

His smile faltered. "How do you know Theresa?"

"She works for Parker. I'm staying at his place for a couple of days."

His eyes widened as a light bulb went off over his head. "You're the sweet young thing that found the body."

One out of three wasn't bad. "Yes, I found her." I remember Greer saying he was going to call Jock as a lawyer for Parker. "Are you representing Parker? Greer said you mostly practice family law."

"I went down and sat with him for questioning, but murder is above my pay grade. A friend of mine, a criminal attorney from Cape Girardeau, is coming up in the morning for his bail hearing."

"How was Parker?"

Jock seemed less asshole-ish when talking about his job. "He was…okay. Freaked out, I think. But who wouldn't be in his situation? The evidence against him is damning. Everyone in town knew Katherine wanted him and his mutts out of Moonrise."

"He didn't do it," I insisted.

Jock's brows went up. "It doesn't matter what we believe. Only what can be proven." He moved in closer to me, and under the citrus smell, I detected vodka, coffee, and a faint whiff of mint and honey. He'd been near enough to Parker to pick up his scent. Jock, his voice low and gravelly, said, "I didn't get your name."

Aaaaaand he was back to being an asshole. I understood now why Theresa was so attracted to Keith. Keith was a gentle soul with a kind heart. Jock was a philandering bully, level expert.

"Her name," Nadine said as she put her finger on his sternum and pushed Jock away, "is Not Interested."

He put his hands up and took two steps back. "You know I like it when you play bad cop, Nadine. If you're jealous, we can always..."

He smirked, and I really wanted to wipe that smile off his face. With my claws. Theresa had told me she and Jock had grown apart because of work and politics, but I think she left out a few details about her errant husband.

"Go away, Jock. I don't know how the hell Theresa puts up with you."

I saw the banked fury in his gaze, but his expression didn't change. He turned and handed me a business card. "If you ever find yourself in trouble, give me a call." He gave another shark-like grin to my friend. "See you later, Nadine."

"Only if I'm unlucky," she said.

"What was that about?" I asked.

"I used to date Jock," said Nadine. "Much to my eternal regret." When I gave her a questioning look, she added,

"No, I don't want to talk about it. Besides, we have other business."

"Get away from me!" the barking order drew my attention. Ed Miles was at the bar arguing with a tall blond man. I tried to hone my hearing to pick up more of their conversation, but there were more than ten people between me and the bar, and they were all whooping it up. Plus, the conversation between Ed and the blond got very quiet. The guy never turned around so I couldn't get a good look at him.

I elbowed Nadine. "Ed's fighting with someone."

She looked toward the bar. "Who? Ralph? Nah. He's just telling Ed he's not getting another drink. It's a nightly ritual with those two."

I looked again and saw that Ed was now talking to the big, burly bartender who appeared to be refusing to serve the older, and very drunk, man.

Huh. Where did the blond guy go?

Ed stumbled off his stool, obviously steamed about being cut off. He staggered a little before somewhat gaining his balance. He weaved through the crowd and headed toward the exit.

Nadine grabbed my forearm. "Let's follow him."

Katherine's brother, jacket on, walked—if you counted bouncing against the walls as walking—down the bathroom hallway and out a door at the end leading outside.

The cold breeze that rushed in raised goose bumps on my arms. "Shoot, we left our coats back at the table."

Nadine nodded toward the door. "You go. Ed's going to the smoker's area out back." She looked at her watch. "We got a couple of minutes."

"It's pretty cold."

"He's got enough antifreeze in him tonight he won't notice."

Getting back to the table, I had a moment of empathy for spawning salmon. A tall sandy blonde at the bar caught my attention. I recognized Freda, Buzz's waitress. She looked exhausted. She looked back over her shoulder as she tapped on the bar. When she saw me, she gave me a quick head wave and a tired smile.

I had a moment of worry. If Lacy was here and Freda was here—who was watching the baby?

Not your business, Lily. I grabbed mine and Nadine's coats and headed back to the hall.

"I just checked," Nadine said. "He's still out there."

We put on our winter gear and braved the evening elements. Four men and six women stood out on the snowed-in patio. They huddled around a large, lit chiminea. One of the guys fed kindling into its belly. The warmth of the fire had melted the snow around the base area, and the women made sure their feet were on the dry spots.

Off to the side, leaning against the wall of the building, stood Ed Miles. He had one hand shoved in his pocket and the other, cradling a lit cigarette. He took a long drag, the cherry lighting up like a beacon as he inhaled. Smoke combined with breath fog, creating a diaphanous veil around his head. I couldn't tell if he was sad about Katherine's death or if depressed drunk was his normal state of being.

I nudged Nadine. We approached Ed, faking nonchalance and failing.

"What do you want?" he groused.

"Howdy, Ed," Nadine said. "Just wanted to tell you how sorry I am about Katie."

Ed snorted and shook his head. He took another drag off his cigarette. "That's rich. There ain't a goll-darn person in this town that ain't celebrating Katie's death like the Fourth of July."

"Even you?" I asked.

Ed gave me a hard look. "I don't know you."

"This is Buzz Mason's cousin. She's visiting."

He tossed the butt on the ground and stubbed it out with the toe of his boot. "Take my advice, girlie. Go back to where you came from. This town is rotten to the core of it."

"Losing a sibling is hard," I said. "It doesn't matter how much distance might be between the two of you."

"You think you know me?"

"I know pain," I told him. "You wear yours like a blanket."

"Did you talk to Katie after she left the diner, Ed?" Nadine asked.

His eyes jumped from me to her. "No."

"We have a witness," I lied. Sorta. "This person saw you arguing with your sister."

"You told the sheriff you hadn't seen Katie since lunch."

"I don't have to talk to you." He shifted his gaze between Nadine and me. "Either of you."

"Don't you want to know who killed Katherine?" I asked. "Or maybe *you* killed her, and that's why you won't help."

He rolled up off the wall and rounded on me. His clenching fist didn't have me too worried. He was drunk, and I'm a Shifter. I could get out of the way.

Nadine didn't know that, though, and she put herself between Ed and me.

"It's all right," I told her. "He isn't going to hit me."

"I didn't kill Katie," Ed seethed.

"Why were you fighting?" Nadine asked.

"She…" He shook his head. "It's too dangerous."

I rose up on my toes as excitement tittered through me. "What is?"

A crash inside the bar, followed by frantic shouts, brought our unofficial interrogation to a screeching halt.

The back door flew open as people pushed their way outside. I could smell the smoke then. Electrical, not wood or cigarette. "There's a fire," I told Nadine.

"I have to get people out safely," she said, pushing her way through the drunks to get back inside.

I followed after her.

Smoke detectors were beeping loudly, but the fire must have affected the electrical system because the lights were out. I heard Nadine shout, "Everybody out! Move."

"The front door is blocked," someone cried.

"Get to the back," Nadine shouted. With my Shifter vision, I could see her pushing people back toward the hall. She'd pulled her shirt up over her mouth, but she coughed even as she barked out orders.

The spray of a fire extinguisher added to the chaos as the room filled with acrid smoke. The bartender was fighting a losing battle with the flames. I grabbed his arm.

"You need to go," I said. "Get out and call the fire department."

The greasy, smoke laden ceiling tiles carried the fire quickly across the ceiling, and the heat went from a five to a five hundred in a couple of seconds.

I yanked him over the bar, not caring that a human my size shouldn't be able to lift a man well over six feet in height and close to three hundred pounds so easily. I helped him to his feet when I had him on the other side.

"Go!" I yelled.

Stupefied, he nodded and took off down the hallway.

I scanned the room and looked for more stragglers. I saw someone on the ground. The thick haze made it impossible to identify the person, but that was irrelevant. I wasn't leaving anyone in a burning building. The acrid smoke choked me. My throat burned and my eyes watered. Even as a Shifter, I couldn't survive the fire much longer. I dropped to the ground and crawled toward the body.

Oh, Goddess. Nadine! My heart turned over in my chest. She was barely breathing, and her pulse was weak. I smelled blood, even over the burning wood and alcohol-soaked floor. I had to get her outside. In my human form, I couldn't drag her and crawl at the same time. Not with any efficiency. I had a half-second debate with myself before I slid out of my large coat and my favorite dress. I was down to my underwear and bra, but I knew those would stay on, even in the shift.

I rolled Nadine on top of my coat, tying the arms under her armpits and across her chest. Next, I tucked my dress inside the coat so I could drag it with me. After, I concentrated on my bones cracking and twisting. I felt my skin give way as fur sprouted down my body. My hands and feet turned to paws, my long torso into a sleek blonde body. The elation of shifting brought a roar to my lips that was distinctly sharp and loud.

I grabbed the knotted coat sleeves between my teeth and dragged Nadine toward the door.

She moaned, and my fear spiked. If she woke up and saw a giant cougar hauling her away, she'd completely freak out. I dug my claws into the wood floors and moved faster. When I got her to the end of the hall, I shifted back to human and untied the coat from Nadine and slipped it on. There was no time to put on the dress, so I shoved it under the coat, giving me the appearance of a six-month pregnant belly, before taking Nadine out the door.

Flashing lights and sirens flashed from the street. The area outside the back door had been deserted. The only movement on the patio was the dying fire from the chiminea. Since no one was around, I picked her up and got as far from the three-alarm fire as possible. I put her down, leaning her against the back wall. I couldn't risk getting her any closer to the EMTs without having to answer some questions. Like, "Are you on steroids?"

Nadine was coughing now, a good sign. She lifted her head, her face dirty with soot and her clothes singed and stained. "What...what happened?" Her voice sounded like a foghorn.

"You passed out," I said. "I need to get you some help. Will you be all right for a minute?"

"Wait." She tugged on the hem of my coat. "I didn't pass out." She shook her head and winced. "Someone hit me from behind."

The smell of blood was stronger now. "Goddess on toast," I said. The assault must've happened when I was rescuing the bartender. There had been too many humans running around, and I hadn't paid attention to any of them. "Who would do that?"

"I don't..." She put her hand on the back of her head. Her fingers came away bloody. "Ow."

Hit in the back of the head. Just like Katherine. I scanned the area, suddenly afraid that Nadine's attacker might be skulking around. I couldn't leave Nadine alone, not even for the minute it would take to retrieve help. "C'mon," I said. I reached down, and she grabbed my arm. "You've got to walk out of here."

Nadine would've toppled me if I hadn't been a Shifter. I grabbed her waist, and she slung an arm around my shoulders.

"You must really work out," she said. "You're part-Hulk."

"All that weight training finally paid off," I said. We started limping out from around the back and down the narrow alleyway between the bar and another building —but we didn't get very far before we saw the man crumpled on the ground.

I recognized the sour smell and the jacket immediately. The rusty scent of blood was overpowering.

"Shit," breathed Nadine. "Who is that?"

I realized she couldn't see the lifeless stare or the mouth frozen in a permanent grimace of horror. We moved closer and bent over to stare at the man's face.

Nadine gasped. She fumbled in her jacket pocket, pulled out her cell phone, and hit a single button. "Sheriff? It's Nadine. I'm down at Nix's Bar, around the back. Yes, where the fire broke out," she said in answer to a question I heard him ask her. "Ed Miles has been murdered."

CHAPTER 14

Blood spatter, like a Jackson Pollock painting, decorated the bar's exterior where Ed had been found. The longest tail was about five feet up the side, indicating he was probably standing when he was killed. His carotid artery had been punctured on the right side, which meant he'd have bled out in a couple of minutes. The hole had been small, the size of an ice pick. Maybe smaller.

Most disturbingly, he'd been killed a few minutes before I managed to drag out Nadine. His wallet had fallen out of his pocket, and I picked it up and did a quick rummage. I realized it was bad form to take potential evidence from a crime scene, but I wanted to look. Impetuously, I tucked his license into my coat.

Could I have saved him if I'd been faster? I pulled my coat tighter and shivered as guilt tugged at my conscience while the medics got Nadine onto a stretcher.

All the evacuated customers and employees were on the far side of the street now in a triage set up by the local hospital, fire department, and EMTs. Ryan Petry was sitting on the sidewalk with an oxygen mask on. Jock Simmons was talking to the bartender and a deputy I recognized from the Katherine Kapersky crime scene. I couldn't find Freda or Lacy in the mix of bodies, but I'd heard a fireman say, "The building is clear, but there was a crowbar wedged under the front door, blocking the exit. We're lucky there aren't any fatalities."

Inside, he meant. Because what happened to Ed Miles might not have been fire related, but it was certainly fatal. Had the fire been set to create a distraction for the purpose of killing Ed? If that was the case, then why had they blocked the front door and not the back? It made no sense if they wanted to get Ed alone to do him in.

Sheriff Avery showed up gruff and angry. I didn't smell burgers and fries on him tonight. From what I could detect, he'd had steamed broccoli, baked chicken, and spinach greens. I suspected that with the sheriff's forced diet, he was more *hangry* than angry.

"What were you thinking, Deputy?" he asked Nadine, who had an oxygen mask on, making the strong, vibrant woman appear frail and fragile. Human. "You're a police officer, not a fireman," the sheriff continued. "You don't go running into burning buildings." Behind the crotchety butt chewing, I could hear the concern in his voice.

"She was a real hero, Sheriff," Nadine said. "There would have been a lot more people injured if Nadine hadn't herded them toward the back exit."

"According to Ralph Mader, she ain't the only person dumb enough to run into a burning building."

"Ralph? The bartender?"

The sheriff narrowed his gaze on me. "Seems you're pretty strong for a tiny thing."

"I lift weights," I said. "The adrenaline rush probably helped, too."

"Uh-huh," he grunted, unconvinced. "And then you discovered Ed Miles' body?" He chewed the inside of his lip. "That's two bodies in two nights, Miss Mason. If I were a superstitious man, I might say you were bad luck. But since I'm not, I'm going to consider you a person of interest."

I gaped at him. "I've only been in town forty-eight hours," I said, incredulous. "I didn't know these people, much less have a motive to kill them."

"Yet, they were murdered not too long after meeting you."

This guy was unbelievable. Did he seriously think I used people's skulls for batting practice?

Nadine pulled the oxygen mask from her face. "I can vouch for her whereabouts, sir. She came in right after me, and Ed was alive when the commotion started."

"Weren't you out for a bit, Deputy?" He looked at me, suspicious. "Could be you and Parker are in on it together," said the sheriff. "He did Katherine, and you did Ed."

"That's your theory? I helped Ralph escape then I ran outside, with more than a dozen other people, tracked down Ed and killed him without being seen. *Then* I ran back inside the building to drag out Nadine?" Where did this guy get his police training? Yosemite Sam cartoons?

I could see that even the sheriff considered that scenario far-fetched, but he was too stubborn to admit it. "Something's off about you, Miss Mason. I don't think it's a coincidence Moonrise had two murders after you got to town."

A very nonhuman chuffing sound caught in my throat as my exasperation hit level ten. I need to refocus his attention on an actual investigation that did not lead to Parker or to me. "Ed said he and Katherine were fighting about something last night. Something that he thought might have gotten her killed. I think he was scared for his own life."

The sheriff harrumphed. "Ed Miles didn't see Katherine after lunch yesterday at The Cat's Meow." He pulled out the notepad in his pocket and tapped the cover. "It's on record."

Apparently, the sheriff had the idea that his notebook carried the same weight as the Ten Commandments. Writing down a lie did not make it true. Hazel had never conveyed how crazy humans were—especially those in law enforcement.

"Ed told us that he saw his sister last night."

"It's true, Sheriff," Nadine said, holding the oxygen mask away from her face. "He was telling us about it when the fire broke out."

"Keep that over your mouth, Deputy. Smoke inhalation is nothing to mess around with." He looked at me, suspicion in his gaze. "And how come you aren't suffering the ill effects of the fire, Miss Mason?"

"Sheriff, are you saying that you'd prefer I'd gotten hurt?" I blinked at him innocently. "I'm truly sorry I didn't get horribly burned or at the very least, try to suffer a collapsed lung."

His face turned a dark shade of red. "Don't leave town," he told me. He nodded to Nadine and then took his leave.

"Collapsed lung?" Nadine laughed, wheezing, and coughed.

"That man has a bug up his butt where I'm concerned," I said to Nadine.

She nodded. "He don't like you much, that's for sure."

"I'm very likable. Some might even call me adorable."

"You grow on people." She grinned. "You know, like a fungus."

I rolled my eyes, but I couldn't help but laugh.

"You get on back to Parker's. Let's meet for coffee in the morning at the diner."

I eyed her. "You think that's a good idea? Aren't you going to the hospital?"

"Nah. I'll be all right. Unless I don't get my morning caffeine. That'll make me homicidal."

"Well, we don't want any more of that around here," I said. "See you in the morning."

"Almighty Christ, Lily. What the hell were you thinking?" Buzz asked for the tenth time since he'd picked me up from the bar. I tried to call for a cab, but apparently, they didn't run at eleven at night.

"No one saw me." When I put my dress on in his backseat, he'd wanted to know why I'd taken the darn thing off in the first place. Which is when I made the mistake of telling him I'd had to shift to get Nadine out of the burning bar. "Did you want me to let her die?"

He scoffed. His knuckles were white as he gripped the

steering wheel. "You don't integrate with humans by sticking your nose in everyone's business."

Now *I* scoffed. "In this town, sticking your nose in people's business seems like a very human thing to do." I slid my coat back on and buttoned it up.

"That's fine for people who have nothing to lose. You draw attention to Shifters, and you're going to find yourself skinned and gutted somewhere. Humans have a tendency to kill first, ask questions late when it comes to things they don't understand."

"No one saw me," I said again. "I'll be more careful, I promise."

He glanced at me. "Did you at least find out anything from Ed?"

"He was scared. Scared about something Katherine had told him. Enough so, he lied to the police about seeing her."

"Do you think the same person who killed Katherine killed Ed?"

"I do." I climbed from the back seat to the front. "I want to go to Ed's place and look around."

Buzz gave me a sharp look. "Are you crazy?"

"The cops probably won't search his home tonight, and I want to see if there is anything there that will tell me why he was terrified. Maybe Katherine gave him something. I know she's blackmailing half the town," I said. "I have a feeling she tried to hit someone who decided to hit back. With Parker's bat."

"You aren't going to let this go, are you?"

I hid a smile. "Nope. So, you can either take me and watch my back, or you can let me take my chances on my own and maybe get caught." I tried to sound contrite. "I'd hate to make things rough for you if I got caught."

"I told you earlier, I don't know where he lives."

"That's okay." I produced Ed's driver's license from my pocket. "I have the address right here."

"Damn," he said, shaking his head. "You are truly your mother's daughter."

ED'S PLACE WAS A SMALL TWO-STORY WHITE HOUSE ON A small corner lot. The yard was neat, a surprise considering who owned it. The house had a fresh coat of paint. Probably done late summer, maybe early fall, before the freeze. I could still smell the pungent chemical aroma. We got out of the car. I looked at Buzz, and he wiggled his fingers at me and said, "Your show, kid. Have at 'er."

We walked around the back. I was startled to find a doghouse near a tree. "Did Ed have a pet?"

"Used to," Buzz said. "A Dalmatian named Fred. He passed away last year."

The doghouse had a fresh coat of paint as well. Had Ed been planning to get another dog or was he trying to keep memories of Fred alive?

"What are the chances his back door will be unlocked?"

Buzz walked up two concrete steps to the door, using the hem of my dress, I turned the knob and opened it up. "Pretty good."

"No one likes a show-off, Buzz."

"Says you." He walked on in.

Inside, we didn't turn on any lights. I watched Buzz's eyes go silvery as it caught minor refractions of light, giving him excellent night vision. I knew my eyes were doing the same thing as I allowed my animal to surface. Just a little. Ed's house was tidy and well-kept. I was not expecting Ed's home to be anything but a mess. Did he clean when he drank? Maybe drunk housecleaning was something I should try if this was the result.

"Is Ed married?"

"He was once. But all that was back before I moved to town," Buzz said. "Rumor mill says his wife ran off. Two years later he was served with divorce papers."

"Did they live here?" Maybe Ed had left everything exactly as his wife left it. I shook my head. Of course, that was ridiculous.

Probably.

"This used to be his folks' house."

Ah. That explained the beige with blue roses velour couch. The house had a distinctly feminine touch, but it wasn't modern by any means.

In the kitchen, I used a paper towel to open his fridge. Beer, cold cuts, cheese slices, mayonnaise, eggs, and milk. No vegetables. Maybe he thought beer was one of the four food groups. I went for the kitchen drawers next.

"What do think he's hiding in the silverware drawer? I'm pretty sure it's hard to kill someone with a butter knife." His arms were folded across his chest. He was obviously not going to help me find clues.

"Well, a fork would do some damage." I pulled out each drawer one by one. Spice packets. Silverware. Cookware. Knives. Pudding packets. "Wow."

"What?" Buzz said, suddenly interested.

"This guy really liked his pudding. There are about twenty boxes in here. Double Fudge. Pistachio. Vanilla. Lemon."

Buzz sighed and rolled his eyes. "Get on with it, girl."

The next drawer had two screwdrivers, a Phillips and a flat head, a ball-peen hammer, pliers, wire cutters, rubber bands, and a stuffed envelope. I pulled out the envelope. At one time it had been white, but age had given it a yellow tint. There were dark smudges at the corners and a small tear in the flap. I took out the contents. It was a stack of pictures. The ones on top were older. A baby, a toddler, a girl...by the time the pictures showed a teenager, I recognized her.

I handed the graduation picture to Buzz. He looked at it, then back to me, his expression befuddled. "Why does Ed have pictures of Lacy Evans in his drawer?"

"Stalking her maybe?"

"Since she was a baby?" he asked.

"Maybe Katherine brought these over. I wonder if this is what they were fighting about last night."

"I think you should talk to Rex."

"The reverend?"

Buzz expression grew grim. "Look. I have a policy of not getting involved. I've already gone way past my comfort level."

"I can't just sit back and let an innocent man be prosecuted based on purely circumstantial evidence."

"Sure, if you want to tell yourself you're on a crusade for truth and justice, I'll play along, but remember, Parker Knowles is human, Lily. You can play with them, but you can't keep them. That's the rules."

"Like you're doing with Nadine?"

"Nadine is a big girl."

"She's my friend."

"No," Buzz said. "She isn't. Your friends are back in Paradise Falls. They're the people who know what and who you are. You will never be able to completely be yourself in a town of humans. If you plan to stick around, you have to get it in your head that you might live amongst them, but you are not one of them."

"I get it, Buzz," I hissed. "You've made your point perfectly clear."

"I hope so," he said. His eyes were suddenly sad. "It's not always lonely. Sometimes, it's really nice being out here on my own. I don't want you to think it's not worth it to try and make a life on your own terms, Lily. It's just…you can never tell anyone your secret. No one can know."

"I know. I have no plans to tell anyone I can shift into a cougar."

"All right. I overheard Katherine shaking down Theresa Simmons at the diner one morning about six months ago. She knew things that Theresa hadn't told anyone but Reverend Kapersky during a private counseling session."

"What? You think the reverend and his wife are in this together?"

Buzz shrugged. "Freda told me that the rev keeps notes about the parishioners he councils. Dollars to donuts that's how Katherine got the dirt on Rex's flock."

"How could the reverend not know his wife was a blackmailer? Not a single soul went to him and told him about Katherine's shenanigans?"

"Fear keeps people silent. And compliant."

"Why would anyone get counsel from the rev if they knew that's where Katherine got her information?"

"Well, now, we don't know for sure how she stole people's secrets. It's just my theory."

"Goddess in a tank top," I whispered. "I can't believe someone didn't kill that woman sooner."

"You and me both."

"Is Freda working in the morning?"

"Yep," Buzz said. "She's off on Wednesdays and Thursdays."

"Good." I tucked the pictures into my coat pocket. "Maybe she'll have some idea why Ed had all these pictures of her daughter."

"If you're done playing Nancy Drew, let's get going. I don't like disrespecting the dead."

"Okay."

By the time Buzz dropped me at Parker's, all the lights in the main house were off. I was bummed that I wouldn't have Smooshie to keep me company during the night, but I didn't want to wake up Greer just so I wouldn't have to sleep alone.

I trudged up the stairs to the apartment, my legs stinging from the cold wind. Mentally and physically, I was exhausted as I let myself into the small loft.

A piece of paper floated along the floor as the outside breeze kicked it around. I closed the door and rubbed my eyes. The note was on a yellow piece of stationary. I could see bold, black letters bleeding through the back side. I leaned over and picked it up. When I turned it over, my pulse quickened, and the blood drained from my face.

Hand printed on the paper was the message, *I know your secret.*

I fought against the urge to turn into a cougar and curl up under the blankets and hide. There hadn't been a demand or threat, but somehow, the note conveyed both. Did this person see me shift in the bar? If he or she did, how would they even know what they'd seen? Did this person know about Shifters? Our existence was secret for a reason.

Was it too late to call Haze? I knew if I asked, she would drop everything to come to my aid. Did wanting my best friend to rescue me make me feeble and pathetic? I'd made the choice to leave Paradise Falls. I wanted a fresh start. If I turned back now, I might never make it out of my hometown again.

In Paradise Falls, I would always be the girl with the murdered family. A victim. I didn't want to be a victim.

I wanted to be a survivor. Survivors didn't call in their witch BFFs to magically fix things.

Buzz had been right about how stupid I'd been at the bar. I understood that now. I'd been so sure of myself. There'd been so much smoke and heat, someone could have been inside, could have seen me, and I would have never known. I'd let my own superior notion of my senses make me cocky.

Fear and adrenaline hindered my ability to think straight. The person who left the note might have left a trace of themselves behind, a clue to his or her identity. I unfolded the crumpled note, my hands shaking as I brought it close to my face to sniff. The bold, black lines held the tart scent of permanent marker. No help there. You could get that kind of marker in any store. There was a faint gumminess at the edge of the upper left corner. There was a hint of a lemony aroma, but not from real lemons. Something artificial maybe. I closed my eyes and inhaled again. And cloves. Like what I'd smelled on Katherine Kapersky.

My heartbeat throbbed in my throat.

Was the note from the killer? Was I next on his or her list?

CHAPTER 15

S unlight filtered through the window, casting its rays across my face. I swatted at the beam of light as if it were an annoying fly.

"Go away," I groaned. I looked at the clock. It was eight in the morning. "Ungh."

I'd slept for three hours, and that wasn't in a row. A sharp bark outside the apartment followed by a series of whimpering whines forced me up from the bed. I slid some leggings on under the night shirt I wore.

I opened the door, a cool breeze smacking me in the face and whipping through my clothes like they were made of cheesecloth, and found Smooshie sitting on the stoop. Her face, paws, and forearms were muddy, and the rest of her was wet. Apparently, my Houdini hound had managed to escape the back fence again. She barked again, barreled around me, jumped onto the bed, and rooted around the messy blankets until she was under them.

I smiled, and until that moment, I hadn't been certain I'd ever smile again. "Good morning, Smoosh." I crawled into bed with her, the covers between us, and wrapped my arms around her. I felt a knot ease in my chest as she huffed out her breath in a contented sigh.

"Let's just stay inside today. What do you say, girl?"

In reply, she shuffled her body in a circle until her head was on my shoulder. She licked my face. "I'm glad you agree."

The person knocking on my door had other plans in mind.

"Just a minute." Smooshie stayed under the covers. I couldn't blame her.

I cracked the door open and peeked out. My pulse picked up the pace.

"Parker."

"Hey, Lily." His dark hair was mussed, and there were dark shadows under his blue eyes. He rubbed his hand through his hair. "I…"

"Come in." I wanted to fling my arms around him, tell him everything would be okay, but I had a feeling that if I allowed myself to get too close, I wouldn't let him go. "I picked up some coffee yesterday. I could make us some."

He gave me a quick, polite smile. "I'd like that."

He sat at the small table in the kitchenette area as I prepared the coffee maker and added water. "I'm glad you're home."

"I was given a bail hearing this morning." He shook his head. "I still can't believe they think I killed her." He stared at me, his eyes penetrating and serious. "You don't think I did it, do you?"

"Of course not," I told him. I took two small white mugs from the cabinet. I thought about the note. My gut twisted at the threat it implied. "I think whoever killed Katherine also murdered her brother Ed. You were in jail at the time so you couldn't have done it."

"Oh." He looked disappointed. "Well, I'm glad you don't think I'm a suspect anymore."

I wished the percolator would percolate a little faster. This was turning into a "must have coffee" conversation. "I never thought you did it." I tapped the counter, willing the slow machine to hurry. "It's why I went out last night. I found out Katherine had a fight with her brother the night she died. I thought he might know something that would point to the real killer."

His mouth was still grim, but the lines in his forehead eased. "What did you find out?"

That someone didn't want me talking to Ed Miles. "Not very much. The fire happened and then…"

"Ed was dead." He shook his head again. "I can't believe this. Why would someone do all this?"

"You can't throw a stone in this town without hitting someone who had a reason to want Katherine Kapersky gone."

Parker chuckled. "True. But that's not what I meant. Whoever killed her went out of their way to set me up for it. Why? I don't get it."

"Do you have any enemies?"

"I haven't had any enemies since I came back from the war." He wrung his hands. "I keep to myself, Lily. I don't interact with a lot of people. Unless they have something to do with the dogs I rescue, I don't generally bother."

"Yeah, I can see that about you." I sat down as the coffeepot hissed and gurgled.

"I'm sorry," he said, picking at a chip in the table's laminate top.

"For what?" I was at a loss for what he could possibly be sorry for.

"Yesterday." He tapped his thumb. "At the jail yard. The way I went after that guy. I...I don't like that you saw me that way."

He was earnest in his apology, which is why I didn't try to minimize his feelings about the situation. But honestly, random violence is the norm in a Shifter community. I'd been exposed to it my whole life. "You were under a lot of stress."

"When that guy talked to you the way he did." He shook his head. "I was wound up pretty tight already."

I decided to broach the subject of his anxiety. He'd brought up the war earlier, so I didn't think it was out of the blue for me to ask. "Do you suffer from PTSD? I mean, from your service?"

He nodded but didn't meet my eyes. "I don't like to talk about it."

"That's all right. We don't have to talk about it." A final hissing signaled the coffee was finished. The aroma of the smooth, dark roast filled the kitchen. I got up and poured us both a cup.

"Elvis saved my life."

He'd said as much at dinner my first night in town, but not how. "Was he a military dog?"

Parker laughed, the mirth brightened his sky-blue eyes. "No." He took the cup from me and put his hand over the top to warm his palm. "I was at BAMC down in San Antonio—"

"Bamsee?" That sounded made up.

He grinned. "Brooke Army Medical Center at Fort Sam Houston. It's an Army base in San Antonio. It's where they sent me after I was patched up to recover."

"Patched up from what?"

"I really hadn't planned to talk about this."

"Up to you." I took a sip of my coffee, the dark, hot caffeine was like manna for my taste buds. I suppressed a groan of pleasure. Maybe that coffeepot was worth the wait.

Parker pushed his chair back a little from the table. "Firefight in Yemen. I took a bullet in my left shoulder and another in the chest. It missed my heart by a few inches."

"Goddess," I whispered. I knew he'd probably seen some awful stuff, but he'd nearly died. "Are you…"

"I'm fine now." He flexed his left hand. "Some weakness in my fingers and I don't have the rotation in my shoulder that I used to have, but other than that it's all healed up."

"And Elvis. Where did he come in?"

"Things got dark for me stateside. My military career was over, and…" He closed his eyes. He shook his head and opened his eyes again. "The nightmares. Not just about getting wounded. It was a mess there. I lost several buddies."

"I'm sorry, Parker."

"A friend of mine wanted to adopt a dog from a kill shelter, and I went with him. Elvis was scheduled to be put down that week if no one adopted him. Two seconds after we met, I knew he was mine. That night, I had the best sleep I'd had in two years. Elvis tucked in on me, and I felt…calm."

I got it. Seriously. Smooshie made me feel the same way. Speaking of. She nudged her nose under my hand. "You decided to get up, eh?" She wagged her tail as I rubbed her shoulders and scratched her lower back. "It sounds like you rescued him, and he returned the favor."

Parker smiled. "You're right. The reason he's so behaved is because we did a training course. He's a certified emotional support dog. Which means I can take him with me to most places."

"But not jail."

He nodded. "Not jail."

"Hence the anxiety and the violent reaction to the douchebag in the yard."

"You nailed it." He reached over and scratched Smooshie under the chin. "I didn't like the way he talked to you." His intense gaze made my insides squishy.

"I…I'm glad you're back home."

"Hopefully, I'll get to stay."

"Well, I've been checking around on the case. I think I have some leads. I don't know if anything will pan out, but I know you didn't do this, and I plan to prove it."

Parker leaned forward and put his elbows on the table. "You should let the police handle the case."

"Because that's worked out so well for you. As far as Sheriff Avery is concerned, he has all the evidence he needs to convict you with that stupid bat. It's ridiculous."

"You better watch it, Lily Mason. You keep talking like that, someone might suspect you like me."

Oh, no. My heart tittered. "I would help anyone I thought was innocent," I protested. Heat crept up to my ears. I was not a virgin, not for many years, so I wasn't sure why Parker made me feel like a giddy school girl. His dark eyelashes swept his cheek as he blinked and it was as if I could see the whole thing in slow motion.

Stop it, I reprimanded myself. *Human.* As Buzz said, I could have fun with them, but there could be no long-term future for Parker and me. The problem was, if I let myself have fun with Parker, I knew I would want to keep him.

"It's all right, Lily Drew," he said, making a Nancy Drew reference. "I'm just teasing you. Seriously, though. I don't want you to get in trouble. Or worse. Hurt because you're trying to help me.

"I'm supposed to have coffee with Nadine Booth this morning at the diner." And I needed to talk to Freda. I had a lot of questions about those photographs I found at Eds. Though, I wasn't going to tell Parker about my clandestine B&E with my uncle last night. "She'll tell me what the medical examiner has to say about Ed."

"Really?"

"Uhm, maybe you better keep that to yourself."

"Will do. I better get down to the shelter. Theresa and the other volunteers all showed up this morning, thank heavens, but I should probably be there."

"Do you want to have lunch this afternoon?"

His face lit up, making him look less exhausted. "Sure. I'd really like that."

"I'll see you at noon then."

"Noon it is."

Nadine had been waiting when I arrived at The Cat's Meow. The tables and booths were full, but she'd saved me a seat at the counter. She wore jeans that flattered her curvy figure and a V-neck black sweater. For a woman who'd nearly died the night before, she looked darn good.

"How are you feeling this morning?" I asked.

"Like dog crap." Nadine coughed as if to emphasize the dog crappiness. "My lungs feel like they've been seared from the inside. I've been coughing up junk since I woke up this morning."

"I've seen dog crap." Right before I arrived, as a matter of clarification. "I can't believe the paramedics let you go home."

Nadine shrugged. "They didn't. The sheriff insisted I go to the hospital. They did a breathing treatment, checked my oxygen levels, and when everything was good, they sent me home with some meds."

"Did you hear anything about how Ed was killed?"

"You don't mess around, woman."

"Life's too short to be indirect."

"Nothing like a couple of murders and a fire to hammer that nail home." She picked at her fingernail. It was the first sign that the fire had shaken the unshakable Nadine. "The medical examiner says Ed died of exsanguination. A small puncture to the right side of the neck."

"I thought the hole could have been made with an ice pick. One from inside the bar, maybe."

Nadine pursed her lips. "No, it can't be an ice pick. The weapon had a curved end."

"Like a hook?"

"Not that curved," she said. "He's running a search through some kind of database to find a match."

"I meant to ask. The alligator clip next to Katherine's

body. Did that have any prints or residue or whatever on it?"

"Alligator clip?"

"Yeah, like they use to pin feathers in hair with."

Nadine smirked. "Oh, you mean a roach clip. There wasn't anything like that logged into evidence."

"It was right by her hand."

"Are you certain?"

"Yes." Had the investigators missed that? Was it still in the snow? It had to be. "It's probably still in Parker's backyard."

The front door opened, and a noticeable hush fell over the diner. I glanced up to see Reverend Rex Kapersky walk inside. His long, thin face was contoured with dark shadows of grief. He shrugged his jacket off and sat at the far end of the counter.

A dull murmur grew amongst the other customers. The reverend didn't seem to notice.

Buzz brought out coffee and a plate of eggs, bacon, and crispy hash browns with a side of sausage gravy and biscuits. He set it down in front of the new widower.

"You hang in there, Rex." He tapped the plate. "On the house."

"Thanks, Buzz."

"When's the funeral?"

"We're holding the visitation on Thursday." His blood-shot eyes became glassy with unshed tears. "Funeral's on Friday."

Freda walked over to Nadine and me. She leaned in and quietly said, "Poor man."

"Yeah," Nadine said. "Katherine was a piece of work, but the rev has always been a nice man. He doesn't deserve this kind of heartbreak."

"No one does," I agreed. It didn't stop loss from happening, though. "I'm glad you made it out of the fire last night."

She knocked over a napkin dispenser, straightened it, then cleared her throat. "Uh, what?"

"Nix's Bar last night. You were there, right?"

Nadine gave me a pointed look that asked, *What are you up to?*

I gave her one right back that said, *Don't mess with my flow.*

"Well, I…" Freda's shoulders pinched. "I only stopped in for a minute. I left before the fire started."

Nadine's back went a little straighter as she focused her gaze on Freda. "So you weren't there when Ed was found?"

Freda nodded solemnly. "No, no. I heard this morning. Just awful."

"Were you friends?" I asked.

The sharp look she gave me could have cut a tin can. "I didn't know him well. He was a customer. That's all." For all her previous vacillations, she sure answered that question quickly.

I knew there wasn't any love lost between Freda and Katherine Kapersky. She'd told me that Katherine had called social services on Lacy. But now I wondered if that same "no love lost" extended to Ed. Why had he had that envelope of pictures in his drawer?

Bridgette Jones breezed into The Cat's Meow with a flourish usually reserved for divas. She made a beeline to Rex. "I'm so glad to see you, Reverend Kapersky."

"Hello, Bridgette."

She had a smug air about her that I hadn't noticed in her before. "I've picked out three songs. 'Amazing Grace,' of course, 'Morning Has Broken'—that song is so beautiful with the right harmonies—and we'll finish with 'Safe in the Arms of Jesus'. It was one of Katherine's favorites."

Rex shook his head. "Whatever you decide is fine." He looked at her and forced a tolerant smile. "I appreciate you volunteering to help."

"Katherine's shoes can't be filled in the choir or in our hearts, but I'll do my best."

He nodded. "I know you will."

"What a toady," Nadine hissed. "Ugh."

"You don't like Bridgette Jones?"

"Can't stand her."

"I'm sensing a past here."

"You're like the Amazing Kreskin," she said sarcastically and wiggled her fingers at me. I had no idea who she was talking about, but I got the gist.

"Ha ha."

"Bridge and I were in the same grade in school. She was a cheerleader, on the student council, the yearbook committee, and dated the quarterback." Nadine nudged me. "That'd be Parker Knowles, by the way."

My stomach dipped. "They dated?"

"Oh, yeah," Nadine said. "For two years. They broke up when she went off to college, and he joined the military. It was quite the drama back then."

I examined Bridgette. She was soft and feminine, with her blonde curls and her heart-shaped face and bee-stung lips. I hated to admit it, but she was a real classic and wholesome beauty. I could see why Parker liked her.

Nadine flicked me to get my attention. "It was a long time ago, Lily. If it makes you feel any better, he's the one who broke things off."

It did make me feel better. "I don't know what you're talking about." I delved into my warm, gooey cinnamon roll and took a large bite.

"Uh-huh, sure," she said. "I don't have to be a psychic to know you got a thing for a certain dog lover."

"So why don't you like Bridgette? I mean specifically."

"Because I wanted to date the high school quarterback."

My mouth dropped open, and Nadine laughed.

"You should see your face! I'm kidding, Lils." She slapped my knee. "She and her pals just made my life difficult is all. Mean comments, that kind of thing. High school antics. I wasn't pretty, popular, athletic, or rich."

"You're beautiful," I told her.

"I've blossomed since high school," she said. "Not exactly ugly duckling to swan, but I don't hate the way I look." Nadine shrugged. "And really, Bridgette has probably changed a lot since we were young, but the sixteen-year-old inside me will probably never forgive the sixteen-year-old her."

"I get it." If it hadn't been for Haze Kinsey, high school would have been a complete nightmare for me. I was small for a Shifter, a runt. There might be some who consider being tiny an asset, but Shifters valued strength above all else. "I have a few errands to run. Do you want to get together later?"

"I think I might have plans with..." She gestured toward the kitchen.

"Ah." I smiled. "Have fun."

She cocked her head sideways and flashed me a conspiratorial grin. "I always do."

CHAPTER 16

A brisk twenty minutes later, I was back at Parker's place. I didn't go inside right away. Instead, I went through the side gate into the backyard. Something Nadine said nagged at me to the point of distraction.

No alligator clip had been logged into evidence.

Sure, it had been night, and the snow was deep, but the clip had been right next to her hand. It should have been easily spotted.

Keith was in the back with a gorgeous black and white pittie named Rocko. He waved as I trekked to the back of the yard toward the fence.

Disturbingly, I could still smell Katherine's blood where it had sieved through the snow and soaked into the ground. I toed the snow around where I'd seen the clip. It wasn't there. I bent over and used my gloved hands to dig up the snow. Still no alligator clip.

"Whatcha doin'?" The low and familiar voice startled me as a large object hit my backside and, already off balance, I fell forward, ungracefully face-planting in the snow and rolled over onto my back.

"Smooshie!" I sputtered, glad that I hadn't landed in the exact spot Katherine had died. The exuberant pittie put her paws on my stomach and licked my face before I could defend myself. I laughed. "Stop it." She had perfected the sneak attack.

After I scratched her chest and gave her ear a cuff, she moved off me to sniff around. Parker held out his hand. I took it, and he hauled me up.

"Did you lose something out here?"

"Maybe." I wasn't sure if it was lost or if someone had taken it. Heck, I wasn't even sure the darn thing was important. "I saw something near Katherine's hand."

His expression grew stark. "What was it?"

"A metal alligator clip. Do you use those here?"

"No. I don't. I can't say whether one of the volunteers might have brought one in." His brow wrinkled. "Maybe a couple of teenagers snuck into the backyard to get high in the middle of the night."

I shook my head. "This was sitting on top of the snow. If it had been there before she was killed, I think it would have been covered."

"Maybe Katherine Kapersky was a secret pothead."

An image of the uptight, well-dressed, and perfectly quaffed woman toking on a doobie flashed in my head. It was horrible of me, but I laughed. "You never know."

"Did you find out anything about Ed from Deputy Booth?"

I blinked at the abrupt change in subject. "He was killed with some kind of pointed half-hook. Does that sound like anything you've ever seen?"

"No." He squinched his eyes. "I can't think of a single weapon like that." Parker yawned, his teeth chattering at the end.

I rubbed my hands together. "It's freezing out here," I said. I looked at Smooshie, who'd just finished squatting to pee. "We should go in."

"What about your evidence?"

"There's nothing more to find out here except a case of frostbite." I looped my arm in his and whistled for Smoosh. "Let's see if there's leftover spaghetti from the other night."

We went inside, Smooshie right behind us. The second we were in the kitchen she had her nose up Elvis' butt.

I gently pulled her back. "Stop that." Her face, a myriad of excitement, made it appear as if she were laughing at me, but she listened and sat beside me at the kitchen table.

"You're in luck," Parker said. He held the refrigerator open, his body angled away from me. He'd taken off his winter coat, and his biceps flexed as he leaned forward. Goddess, he was handsome.

Parker blew out a long breath and grinned as he grabbed a covered plastic bowl and set it on the counter. "Hot or cold?"

"There are options?"

"I personally like it cold on bread with some butter, but my dad likes it cold on bread with mayo."

"Like a sandwich?"

"Yes." Parker laughed at my incredulity. "It tastes better than it sounds."

"I certainly hope so." I licked my lips and nodded. "Why not? I'll take a cold spaghetti sandwich."

Surprisingly, the cold spaghetti sandwich was delicious. Tangy and buttery and *mmm-mmm* good. It definitely hit the spot. When we finished lunch, Parker opened the fridge to put the food away and knocked a bottle of pinkish-brown liquid onto the floor. It busted, and a chunk of brown glass slid across the linoleum. I stood up, and Parker held out his hand.

"Careful now."

The scent was acrid and medicine-like with some kind of alcohol base. "What is that?" My werecougar senses could barely handle the pungent aroma.

"It's some medicine that Doc Petry gave me for Luke, the brindle pittie that I took in last week."

"Oh." I pinched my nose. I remembered Ryan Petry from Nix's Bar. To be more precise, I remembered his fine backside. "What for?"

"Poor thing came to me with stomatitis. I have to swab the chlorhexidine over the ulcers on his gums along with antibiotics to clear up the infection."

As he cleaned the mess, the solution smelled less like medicine and more like alcohol. I scrunched my nose and forced myself to inhale deeply. I'd smelled that scent before.

My stomach squeezed. It was similar to the alcohol I'd smelled on Katherine Kapersky. Was this more evidence against Parker? Or someone who worked at the shelter? Or maybe Dr. Petry had some involvement in the crime.

Theresa Simmons walked into the kitchen, a folder of papers in her hand. Her boots were wet with snow, but she'd dropped her coat at the door. She stopped, startled when she saw Parker stooped over the mess with a wet rag in his hand. "Do you want some help?"

"No," he said. "I'm good."

I noticed she had bruises on her right wrist, and her makeup was applied a little heavier on the left side of her face. Bile churned in my gut. I'd met her jerk of a husband the night before. Had he hit her? Was that another reason they weren't getting along?

She smiled at me. "Afternoon, Lily. It's nice to see you again."

I smiled back. "You too, Theresa. How are you today?"

Her eyes clouded, and she said, with only the slightest hesitation, "I'm great. Thanks for asking."

Was Jock Simmons a violent man, on top of being a womanizer and all-around douchebag? I remembered Theresa saying how unhappy he became after Katherine Kapersky was elected president of the town council. Had he finally had enough of solely venting his rage at Theresa and turned his attention to the woman who usurped his place of power?

I asked, "Did Jock make it out of Nix's unharmed last night?"

I watched the thoughts in Theresa's head stagger at my abrupt question. "What…I… Yes, I guess so."

"There was a fire there last night," Parker said. "Someone lit the place up and killed Ed Miles."

"Jesus," Theresa hissed. "I hadn't heard."

"It's all over town," a robust man about five-nine in height with a jolly round face said. Larry Davis, one of Parker's volunteers. I'd met him the day before.

"I haven't watched the news this morning," Theresa said in her defense. "I've been at home working on the shelter's bills today."

"For which I am most appreciative," Parker said.

I said. "I thought maybe the sheriff might have told you." She was his daughter, after all.

Theresa shook her head. "I'm going to go and file these back in the office," Theresa said. She gave Parker a pointed look. "We need more cleaning supplies. I'll add it to our donation list on the website."

"You're the best," he said.

Her expression warmed at his appreciation. "Thanks."

When we were alone, I glanced at Parker, who was wringing out the washcloth in the sink. He turned to me as if he could feel my stare at his back. "What?"

"Someone is knocking that woman around."

"No." He tucked his chin, the corners of his mouth turning down in a frown of denial. "She's fine."

Was he really this oblivious? "You've never seen bruises on her before?"

He appeared genuinely baffled. "Nothing out of the ordinary.".

I could tell Parker believed what he was saying. Maybe I was reading the situation wrong. Or maybe, Jock being a wife beater was the reason Katherine Kapersky was able to keep the man under her thumb. A family law attorney with domestic violence on his record might as well disbar himself.

After lunch, Parker's dad called to say my truck was fixed and ready to go. I could barely contain my excitement. I mean, I'm the kind of girl who usually likes to walk when I can, but the arctic weather made the activity unpleasant at best.

"Do you want me to run you over?" Parker asked.

"I've had my quota of people trying to run me over this week," I replied.

Parker laughed. "I suppose you have."

I shook my head. "I can get myself there. I'll take Smooshie. Maybe take her on a ride around town. I'd like to do a little sightseeing around Moonrise, I think."

"After everything you've had to see and deal with the past couple of days, I wouldn't be surprised if you weren't planning your escape."

"You're still here," I said. His eyes softened. My heart skipped a beat. And I immediately wished I could take it back. "Besides, the sheriff has given me clear orders not to leave town."

"Then I guess you'd better stick around." He stepped in close enough that I could feel the heat of his skin. For a moment, his bright blue eyes met mine. I held my breath, my eyes closing as he gently touched my cheek with his fingertips.

"Lily," he said, his voice hoarse.

I opened my eyes. "I…" Smooshie, thankfully, pushed

her body against my leg and whined, snapping me from my delusion. I stepped back from him and grabbed my coat from the hooks next to the front door. I smiled as if I weren't about to let him kiss me. "I'll see you in a little bit."

With Smooshie's leash in hand, I fled (no exaggeration) from Parker Knowles.

CHAPTER 17

I barely felt the cold on the brisk walk to The Rusty Wrench. A few times Smooshie protested her inability to explore, but I worried that if I stopped, it would give me time to think about what almost happened. I liked Parker. Too much. Which meant, I needed to keep my distance.

My uncle's words kept playing in my brain. *"Parker Knowles is human, Lily. You can play with them, but you can't keep them. That's the rules."*

Growing up in a town full of paranormals, never having to hide who I was, had not prepared me to go out in the world of non-parakind. The boundaries were blurring in an alarming way. Being a Shifter in a human world was harder than I ever imagined. Did I really think I could live beside them and happily watch them, detached and separate? I'm not sure what I'd thought when I left Paradise Falls, but whatever illusions or fantasies I may have harbored, they were now shattered.

Greer met me out front with my keys in his hand. "She's running like a champ now."

Martha the truck looked older somehow. It disturbed me to realize that the few days I'd spent in Moonrise had already started coloring the way I looked at the world. I tugged Smooshie's leash as she sniffed around the asphalt then planted her nose directly in Greer's crotch.

The older man jumped back and laughed. "Well, hello to you too," he said.

"Sorry about that." I took the keys. "How much do I owe you?"

"Forty-eight even," he said.

I tilted my head and met his gaze. "What about the twenty-five for labor?"

"I figure the way you've stood by my kid the last couple of days, I could throw the labor in as a thank you."

I quirked a smile at him. "Giving away service isn't going to keep you in business."

He chuckled, and it reminded me of Parker's laugh. "I've got plenty, missy. Don't you worry about me."

"You sure?"

"Yep." He gestured to the truck. "Now get going. I have an engine to overhaul."

Impulsively, I gave him a quick, awkward hug and ignored the happily baffled expression on his face. "Thanks, Greer."

I opened the driver's door, and Smooshie jumped in as if she'd been riding with me for years. She climbed over to the passenger seat and sat down, her tongue dangling a good six inches out of her opened mouth as she panted with excitement.

I scratched her ear as I scootched in behind the wheel. "You like a good road trip, don't you, girl?"

She barked in response. I put the key in the ignition and fired it up. Martha immediately started, her engine humming. I didn't even smell the telltale sweet smell of leaking antifreeze. Greer Knowles might not be a witch, but what he did with my truck was nothing short of magic. I gave the horn a bump and Greer, who didn't look up from the car he was working on, waved back at me. One cool dude. Parker came from good stock.

I avoided the treacherous four-way by exiting on the side street. The white crust of melted rock salt discolored the asphalt. Martha's wheel wells were already rusted, the hazard of being an old vehicle in a cold region, so I wasn't worried the salt would do more damage. The speed limit was twenty-five down most the streets. The main drag had a few sections that went as high as thirty-five. I followed Main Street until I saw a green sign pointing left that said, "Two Hills Community College – Home of the Beavers." I snorted a laugh and glanced at Smooshie.

"I think Tizzy might like a college full of beavers." Tizzy, Hazel's familiar, had a thing for beaver Shifters. Talk about bad romance.

The pittie wagged her tail, and it made a clunking sound as it slid across the back of her seat and hit the door panel several times. She looked around, her body vibrating with eagerness. As if an invisible hand guided me, I pulled into the nearest lot and found a visitor parking space. The small campus was mostly long, one-story buildings with names like Anne R. Langtree Learning Center and Robert John Blackwell Technical Center. The sidewalks were salted and scraped clean, creating a maze of gray concrete in the fluffy white snow. Students with backpacks and satchels walked between buildings, their coats up around their ears, their heads down as they made their way to classes. With only Smooshie as my witness, I admitted, if only to myself, I was jealous.

A knock on my window startled me. Smooshie began barking. I recognized the shiny brown hair and symmetrically perfect features of the local veterinarian, Ryan Petry.

"Hush, Smoosh." I scratched her neck and shoulder with one hand and rolled the window down a couple of inches with the other. "Can I help you?"

"I thought you might need some help," he said. "You lost? The campus can be confusing to navigate the first time around."

"I'm not lost," I told him since it wasn't a metaphorical question. "I'm just looking."

"The admission's building is the one on the left over there." He pointed to one of the smaller buildings.

"I'm not enrolling. Really, I just pulled in to rest for a moment."

"Do I know you?" he asked. He smiled, and it was breathtaking. I bet a whole lot of women fell helpless at his feet.

"I'm not from around here."

"Still, I feel like I've seen you before."

I decided to let him off the hook. "I was at Nix's last night."

He snapped his fingers. "That's right. You were with Nadine Booth." He gave me a crooked grin. "Wild about that fire."

"Yeah, it was something else." Smooshie crawled over my lap and pushed her nose against the crack in the window. Petry put his hand to her lips, and Smooshie licked his fingers. "Traitor," I said out the side of my mouth.

"Hey, girl," he said. "I see you found a partner in

crime." He glanced at me. "I immunized her and spayed her for Parker Knowles. Are you fostering or adopting?"

"She's adopted me," I said.

"I'm Ryan Petry."

Now I smiled. "I know." I shook my head. "Parker told me about you, and Nadine pointed you out last night. I'm Lily." I rolled down my window about halfway and backed Smooshie up.

"Glad to meet you, Lily." His green eyes shined like polished jewels in the afternoon sun.

"Me too," I replied automatically. "I mean, it's nice to meet you."

"I know what you meant."

"Did you leave before the fire started?"

"I was inside." He shook his head. "I assisted a few ladies who'd had too much to drink."

"A real hero, eh?"

He laughed. "Nothing like that. One of the girls was really out of it. Her friends couldn't get her up from the booth."

"Which one?"

"Her name's Lacy. She's a regular at Nix's."

Lacy had definitely been buzzed and giddy when I'd

seen her, but she'd been far from pass-out drunk. "Wow. I didn't think she'd had that much to drink."

"She couldn't walk." He pursed his lips and shook his head. "I tried to get her out the front door near the booth, but it wouldn't budge. I had to carry her out the back." He put his hand on the roof of the truck at the top of my window, exposing his forearm. I could see some singed hairs around his wrist. He had gotten dangerously close to the flames.

"Where did you first see the fire?"

He squinted his eyes and looked up for a moment then said, "Near me, I think. Over by the pool tables. It happened really fast, and there was all that smoke."

"Well, I'm glad you got out safe."

"You too." He glanced at his watch. "Better go. I got a class in five minutes."

"You teach?"

"Veterinary Clinical Pathology Methods."

"That sounds like a mouthful."

"It's a requirement for the Veterinarian Technology degree the school offers."

"You better get going then."

He hesitated. "Would you like to go out with me?"

"I don't even know you."

"That's why I want to take you on a date. So you can get to know me."

Ryan Petry was handsome, charming, and likable, but he wasn't Parker Knowles. Maybe that was a good thing. "Maybe."

He grinned. "That's not a no."

I started the truck up again and put it in gear. "Don't be late. Minds to shape and all."

"Where can I find you?"

"Bye." I smiled and waved as I backed the truck out the parking spot. It had been a while since my last date, and I wasn't sure how to proceed with a human. "It shouldn't be this complicated, Smoosh."

She curled in the seat and started licking her butt.

"Not helpful," I told her. Unsurprisingly, she didn't care.

After more driving around, I found myself parked out in front of Rex Kapersky's church. There was only one car in the parking lot, a red four-door sedan—an upscale model. Something I imagined Katherine Kapersky would have been proud to drive. The sign over the church's front door proclaimed, *All are welcome*. I hooked Smooshie's leash on her collar. "Last time I checked, you were an *All*," I told her.

Smooshie pulled me up the steps, ready to explore a new place. The doors, like last time, were unlocked.

There wasn't any music today. The church had a quiet serenity that can only happen when a sanctuary was vacant. Absent of activity. I sat in the last pew and Smoosh parked herself between my knees, her head on my left thigh. The interior was a mixture of dark wood grains, rich red and gold fabrics, and stain-glassed windows on both walls. A podium stood at the center of the stage where the choir had been rehearsing just two days earlier. Towering behind the podium on the wall was a statue of Jesus Christ, his hands out as if asking for a hug. I thought it was nice. Some images I've seen of Christ, especially the crucifixion ones, could scare the bejeezus out of people. I sat quietly for a moment and stared at a stained-glass angel.

Reverend Kapersky, wearing black slacks and an untucked white button-down shirt, walked out through a side door at the front of the church. The door I'd seen him go come out of when he greeted Lacy Evans. His shoulders slumped, and his arms were slack as he crossed to the front of the church. Even in the poor lighting, I could see puffy redness around his eyes. His grief was real, and the fact that some people were glad his wife was dead, no matter how awful she might have been, struck a nerve with me.

He turned toward the back of the church and made his way down the middle aisle. His eyes widened when he finally noticed me.

"Can I help you?"

Smooshie popped up and put her paws on the back of

the pew in front of me. "Sorry," I said. I moved her back to the floor.

"All God's creatures, great and small," the reverend said. He walked back to where I sat. He approached us with enough caution for me to count him as a smart man. He held up his hand to Smooshie and let her sniff him. When she pushed her head forward, he took that as permission to pet her. "Beautiful animal."

"Thanks." I kept a tight hold on her leash in case she decided to get aggressive with her affection. "She's a lover," I warned.

Reverend Rex sat next to me and leaned over to pet Smoosh again, and he ended up with a wet lick across his mouth and nose for his effort. He sputtered then wiped his face with the back of his hand and smiled. "Definitely a lover."

"I'm sorry about your wife."

The smile faded. "Thank you." He looked at me. "Did you know Katherine well?"

I shook my head. "No. Really, I didn't know her at all. I…I just…" I realized he didn't know I was the one who had found her.

"It's okay, child." He put his hand on my shoulder. "I thank you for your sympathy. Would you like some counsel, or would you rather me leave you alone to pray?"

I had a million questions to ask the reverend, but I couldn't think of a single organic way to go about it. Buzz had said that some of Katherine's information had to have come from the private counseling sessions between the reverend and his flock. Could that be my way in? After all, Kapersky had offered. "I don't want to be alone."

"Let's go back to my office." He stood and straightened the tail of his shirt.

I followed him back, the heavy scent of musk and alcohol wafting behind him. Some kind of aftershave. At least he hadn't stopped grooming. That was always the first sign of someone who has given up. He ushered me into a room that was maybe twelve feet by ten feet, not quite a square. A large oak desk took up a big chunk of space opposite the door. A wooden office chair with leather padding was situated behind the desk. The reverend sat down and gestured for me to take one of the two hardwood chairs across from him. One wall had a bookshelf filled with different Bibles, like King James, New American Standard, and the International Bible.

"Please have a seat."

He sat with his hands folded on the desk. No pen or paper at the ready. "Do you take notes during your sessions?"

The question surprised him. "If you're worried about confidentiality, you needn't. I no longer take notes." He leaned forward, smiling. "How can I be of service, Miss…?"

"Mason," I told him. "Lily."

"Miss Mason." Some of the kindness and sadness had left his tone. It had been replaced with suspicion and a simmering of anger. "You're the young woman who found Katherine, aren't you?" Before I could deny it, he added, "The sheriff told me your name."

"I'm sorry. I wasn't trying to hide that from you." I walked to the bookshelf.

"Yes, you were." He didn't sound angry. "I don't blame you, Miss Mason."

I pulled out a leather-bound book, thin, almost fragile in its years, from the lower shelf. It smelled of dust, mold, and cardamom.

"Careful, there," the reverend said. "That's a *Taverner's Bible*. Not a first edition, of course, but still pretty rare."

"It's beautiful," I said and slid it back into place. "You have a lot of Bibles." I carefully placed the old tome back in its spot. "You really have a lot of Bibles."

"I believe in studying the whole word," he said. "And since all versions of the Bible have slightly different ways to interpret the original texts, I try to read them all."

On an upper shelf, I saw an *Aramaic to English Bible*. "Isn't Aramaic the original language of the sea scrolls, or something like that?" I remembered the word from a documentary I'd watched, but I hadn't paid enough attention to it to really know.

The reverend smiled. "Something like that."

I tilted the Bible toward me. A picture slid off the shelf and onto the floor. I picked it up. It was a studio photograph of Lacy Evans and a baby in a blue onesie.

"Leave that," the reverend said.

I turned the photo over. In messy cursive, "Our Son, 3 Months Old," was written on the back. Shock took the breath right out of me. "Oh, my God. Are you the father of Lacy Evan's baby?"

"No."

"Do you know who is?"

"That's none of your business, Miss Mason. I would no more share Lacy's confidences than I would yours."

"But your wife didn't have the same compunction, did she?" Smooshie sat down next to me, her head swinging from me to the rev. She obviously felt the tension because she offered a pitiful whine. The reverend's face reddened, but he didn't deny it. I pushed a little harder. "She was reading your private notes, gathering information on people in the church and using it as leverage. Is that why you stopped writing down your sessions when counseling people?"

He rubbed his hands over his face and looked out the

window. I slid the picture in my pocket before he turned back to me. "Katherine wasn't an easy woman, but I loved her. Why did Parker kill her? Over some dogs?"

"He didn't do it." I was beginning to feel like one of those six-second looped videos all over social media. *He didn't do it. He didn't do it. He didn't do it. *insert parrot squawk**

He looked at me, his stare hard as the vein in his forehead pulsed. "Sheriff Avery says he has a solid case against the young man. I hear he suffers from mental problems. I'll be sure to pray for him. I'm a man of God. I have faith that all things happen for a reason."

"Do you really believe God approved a killing spree in Moonrise?"

"That's not what I meant, and you know it."

"Who told you something that was worth killing for?"

"No one." I couldn't detect any deception in Reverend Kapersky. It made me wonder if he was telling the truth or if he was just that naive.

"I've known people who have killed because it was Thursday."

"Then you've known some depraved people, Miss Mason."

"So have you, Reverend. Difference is, I am aware."

CHAPTER 18

The Cat's Meow was closed on Tuesday evenings. I hated to bug Buzz on his night off, but I needed Freda's address. The picture of Lacy and the baby stashed in the rev's Bible might have nothing to do with Katherine's or Ed's deaths, but that same picture had been in Ed's utility drawer. I needed to know why. Buzz gave me the information I wanted with very little guff. Before I hung up, I heard distinct and recognizable giggling in the background. "Tell Nadine I said hello."

"Will do," Buzz said in farewell then hung up.

Freda's home was on the south side of town. As I drove into her neighborhood, the houses decreased in size, but the yards were neat, no clutter anywhere. Many front lawns had skeletons of trees and shrubs with a few evergreens adding pops of color in the snow. I bet the area was real pretty when the flowers were in bloom.

Freda lived on 543 Spring Street. Her house was a pale gray-blue with black shutters, the decorative kind bolted to the siding for show only. She had a one-car paved driveway, and her white station wagon was parked in the space. I pulled onto the side of the road just past her mailbox.

I wasn't sure what I planned to accomplish by visiting Freda. I had my own doubts about whether I was investigating or just being nosey. For one, I had no idea if or how Lacy played any role in Katherine's death. Being a frazzled mom didn't make a person homicidal.

Smooshie practically dragged me to Freda's front door but stopped just shy to pee next to a juniper bush. The mahogany door was charmingly rustic with a speakeasy opening at the top behind a black rod iron grill. I pressed the doorbell and waited. I could hear the soft shuffle of footsteps on the other side then the squeak of a slide bolt on the door. The speakeasy opened. Freda stared at me through the square hole. "Well, hi, Lily. Just give me a sec." She closed the lookout and unlocked the deadbolt and the door handle. She opened the door and look at Smooshie, eyes wide. "Oh, I didn't realize you had your dog with you. I'm really sorry, but I'm allergic. I can't let you in with her."

"That's all right, Freda. I don't want to take up a lot of your time."

"What can I do for you?"

I wasn't sure the best way to approach the subject. I reached into my coat pocket for the picture I'd taken from the church and held it out to her.

"Where'd you get that from?" She took the wallet-sized portrait from me. "Lacy got those done at the studio in the Walmart." She flipped it over, blanching as she read the inscription. She stared at me, her eyes lit with accusation. "Where did you get this from?"

"I found it," I lied.

Freda's expression was guarded now. "I thank you for returning it. Good day, Lily."

I didn't give her time to shut the door on me. "Does Lacy have a connection to Ed Miles?"

"Why are you asking me about Ed?"

How freaked out would Freda get if I told her about his picture stash? "Were they lovers? Was Ed Paulie's father?"

Freda blanched. "That's... No. No. That's not possible." She didn't say it as if in denial. She said it as if she knew for a fact.

Another reason for Ed having all those photos dawned on me. "Was Ed Lacy's father?"

"You need to mind your own business, Lily." Freda swallowed hard, her right hand balled into a fist as she shook her head. "What game are you playing at?"

"I'm not playing, Freda. I'm trying to find out who killed Katherine Kapersky and framed Parker Knowles."

"I don't know anything about that woman's death."

"You're afraid, Freda. It's written all over you. Are you worried Lacy had something to do with Katherine's murder? Maybe she killed Ed too? I did see her at the bar last night."

"You have no right," Freda hissed. She pointed a long, thin finger at me. "Katherine got what was coming to her, but Lacy had nothing to do with it. She was at my house that night. Paulie had a bad case of colic, and she couldn't cope on her own. And as far as killing Ed…" Freda shook her head. "She wouldn't."

"Because he's her father?"

Freda's shoulders slumped, and she leaned against the doorframe. "Don't suppose it matters now. He *was* her father."

"Does she know?"

"I…I don't think so. But she and Ed were always on friendly terms. He was married when I got pregnant with Lacy. He wasn't going to leave his wife, and I wasn't going to get an abortion, so we parted ways. He gave me money over the years in return for my silence."

"You blackmailed him?"

She grimaced. "The arrangement was Ed's idea. I

wouldn't have told his wife. They never had any children, so I think he just wanted to be a part of Lacy's life
in some way. When Sheila left him about five years
later, I didn't want him back. He'd started drinking
pretty heavy, and I was content to leave things as they
were."

"Did Katherine know about Lacy?"

"That old bat didn't know jack crap or she would have
found a way to use the information against me."

"And what about the father of Paulie?"

Freda shrugged. "Honestly, I don't know. I've tried to
get Lacy to tell me, but she refuses."

"You think he's married?"

"I think it's likely."

I nodded. "I appreciate you talking to me, Freda."

"You won't tell anyone. About Ed, I mean."

"No," I assured her. "Not if it doesn't have anything to
do with the killings."

LACY EVANS MIGHT NOT BE A MURDERER, BUT I WAS
beginning to believe she was somewhere at the heart of
these killings. Other than the accident, I hadn't really
had a chance to talk to the woman. She worked as a
legal secretary for Jock Simmons, so I looked up the

lawyer's office and headed down there under the guise of wanting to discuss Parker's case with the man.

I'll admit, I wanted to check his knuckles for bruising as well. I worried for Theresa, and I didn't know what I'd do if it turned out Jock was hitting her. Make no mistake, I would do something. I already didn't like the guy on principle, if it turned out he was a woman beater as well as a douche-nozzle, I might have to mete out some Shifter justice on his abusive butt.

Simmons Family Law was located in the Birch Hills Business Plaza. The long building had a real estate company, a chiropractor, a massage therapist (I made note of the phone number for later), a physical therapist, and a place called The Smile Factory.

I parked out in front of the law office. It was 4:30 in the afternoon, and the sign on the door said they were open until 5:00 p.m. I didn't see Lacy's black sedan, no surprise there since she'd wrecked it, but there was a rental car in the first parking spot.

Smooshie whined when I shut off the engine, and I had a real "oh crap" moment. I couldn't, or should I say, wouldn't leave her in the truck. I didn't know how long my conversation with Lacy would take, and I didn't want to leave Smoosh to her own devices. I'd already seen what she could do with a small office. My truck wasn't much, but I liked my seats and console intact.

I had another "oh crap" moment when Parker pulled into the parking lot next to me. He met my gaze the moment he came to a halt and gave me a thin-lipped smile.

Shoot. I hadn't meant to run away from him or hide from him all day (yes, I had). Elvis was in the seat next to him. Smooshie barked and yipped then smashed her face against the passenger window, her tongue creating streaks in the condensation from her heated breath.

Parker's thin smile turned into a real one as he shook his head. I scratched Smooshie's back. "Good girl," I said gratefully.

Parker got out of his truck and walked to the driver's side of mine. I rolled the window down. "Hey, you." The scent of mint and honey wafted in at me.

"Hey, you," he said. "Watcha doing here?"

"I could ask you the same thing."

"I have an appointment with a lawyer."

"Oh, right." Duh! "I wanted to check in on Lacy and see how she was doing. Ryan told me she passed out during the fire at Nix's."

"Ryan?"

"That veterinarian of yours."

"When did you meet him?"

"He was at the bar last night, and I ran into him over at the college today."

To say my senses were off is an understatement. For example, I hadn't noticed the slight mottling of color in Parker's cheeks, the slight tremble in his fingers, or the quickening of his pulse and breath. But when I said, "Ryan seems like a really nice guy," Elvis wedged himself between Parker and my truck, creating a larger space between us.

I must have looked like a deer caught in the headlights as my eyes widened and my mouth dropped open. I made an "uh" sound, then closed my mouth.

"I'd like you to come in with me, if you want," was not what I thought he'd say, but he did.

I nodded mutely and did a whole bunch of blinking as I grabbed Smooshie's leash. "Do you think Simmons will be okay with me bringing her inside?"

"He has to let Elvis in, I don't see how one more dog will make a difference." His nostrils flared, and I swear his ice-blue eyes turned almost azure.

Lacy Evans was startled to see Smooshie and me show up with Parker. She wrinkled her nose at me then glared at Parker. "You're late."

"You can bill me," Parker said.

She had dark circles under her eyes, and her brunette hair lacked shine and bounce. I could still smell smoke on her. She hadn't showered since last night. "Go on back. He's waiting for you."

"I'll wait out here for you," I said to Parker.

"All right," he said, but I saw the disappointment on his face, and it crushed me.

I wanted to speak to Lacy alone, but not at the expense of Parker's feelings. "Wait up." Smooshie and I met him at the open office door. "I want to go in with you."

"Sure," he said. A muscle in his jaw unclenched. "I'm glad. Dad offered to come, but I think his nerves would just make mine worse." More quietly, he offered, "You have a real calming effect on me, Lily Mason."

"I'm glad." A woozy joy swept over me. Ugh. Stop it.

Jock Simmons said, "You going to stand out there all day or are you coming in?"

Jerk. I searched for the telltale signs of a fight, but his knuckles, along with his nails, were pristine. Maybe he hit her with something other than his fists. Even if he didn't use his wife as a punching bag, he made my Shifter alarms go off. This guy was a baddie.

His eyebrows rose as he recognized me. "You," he said. "You're Nadine's friend."

And you're the cheating scum who beats your wife. I nodded and said, "Yep."

Parker gave me a look that said, "Do you know everyone in town?" We took the two seats across from Jock. Elvis sat calmly and quietly next to Parker, while Smooshie stood between me and the large desk, panting hard while her tail knocked out the "William Tell Overture" against the hardwood.

I bit my lower lip and pretended she wasn't creating a ruckus.

"Let's get down to it," Jock said. "I'm sorry to say, but your case is going to court. I've conferred with Michael Barnett, the lawyer from Cape Girardeau. He will meet you in my office on Thursday to take over your case. The evidence is circumstantial against you, but it was strong enough for the judge to deny the initial dismissal paper. Barnett is better at assessing whether a jury or a judge trial will benefit you the most. With a pile of circumstantial evidence, my bet is he will suggest going with just a judge, but considering the case, I think a jury of your peers might be sympathetic."

In other words, Jock Simmons thought a jury might find Parker "not guilty" because the person he was accused of killing was an unlikeable human being. On one hand, I was glad the news wasn't completely dire, but on the other hand, I was annoyed that this man actually believed the victim wasn't worth justice. I wanted Parker off the hook for Katherine Kapersky's murder more than anything right now, but she was still a person, and her husband would miss her even if nobody else did.

I knew my own baggage was coloring my thoughts. The police in my town had considered my brother trash. They believed because of his ties to some drug activity in town that he'd somehow brought his death on himself. It turned out his murder had nothing to do with drugs, but even if it had, he deserved to have someone give a damn that his life had been snatched away from him before his time.

I took a deep breath, trying to rid myself of the anxiety building in my chest. This wasn't Paradise Falls, and Katherine Kapersky wasn't my brother. Parker was the only person who mattered right now, and his innocence was the only thing I should be thinking about.

Smooshie started to circle the carpet. "Uh-oh."

"Better take her outside," Parker said.

CHAPTER 19

The wind kicked up as I walked Smooshie behind the building to what I hoped was a patch of grass and not a snow-covered concrete pad. I didn't have any plastic bags with me, so wherever the poop landed it was staying. I looked around conspiratorially. We were alone. "Go at it, girl."

Smooshie went to the end of her leash and began circling the snow. Potty was imminent.

I heard the shuffling of footsteps on the sidewalk. The stride was too short to be Parker. Tom Jones rounded the corner of the building seconds later. The genuine shock on his face mirrored my own surprise.

"Hey," he said. "What are you doing here?"

"A friend had an appointment." I didn't say what friend or with whom he had the appointment. I didn't figure it was any of Tom's business. "What are you doing here?"

"The Smile Factory is my office," he said, giving me a white, toothy grin. I noticed then he had something in his right hand. When he spotted me staring, he held out his palm. He held a cigarette. "Caught me."

"I didn't know you smoked." I hadn't smelled it on him during any of our encounters.

"I don't." He held it up then rolled it between his fingertips. "Not anymore. It's been about a year now, and I sometimes miss the routine of smoking." He laughed. "It's dumb, but I just like to come out and pretend to smoke."

"It's not dumb," I told him. I understood the comfort of routine, and how disruptive life could be without it. Smooshie dropped a hot steamy pile that quickly melted down into the snow leaving a brown hole in its wake. I winced. "Sorry about that. I...I don't have anything to pick it up."

Tom wagged the unlit cigarette at me. "You don't tell on me, and I won't tell on you."

"Deal." Smooshie curled up against the outside of my thigh, and I gave her a quick pat. "Have they got any suspects for last night?"

"What do you mean?"

"You know, for Ed's murder."

"Oh, yeah, no. No one yet." He put the cigarette to his

lips and let it dangle. "It was pretty chaotic. I suppose everyone at the bar is a suspect." He pushed his glasses up his nose with his right hand. The imprints on his nose were pretty deep, which meant they were heavy lenses.

"You can't wear contacts?"

"My eyes are sensitive. They look like two pools of blood with irises in the middle after two hours."

"Yikes."

He wore a white lab coat with two waist pockets and Dr. Tom Jones, D.D.S., P.C. embroidered on the right breast panel. He slid the cigarette into his left pocket. "I'm glad you and Nadine made it out of Nix's last night before the fire got you. I saw you pull her out the back door. You're pretty strong for a woman. Especially a tiny thing like yourself."

"Uhm, thanks." I guess. Why hadn't he offered to help me? Was he the note writer? Had he seen me in my cougar form and was saving it for a rainy day request? Maybe he was just the kind of man who didn't put himself in harm's way if he could help it. "I wonder if they figured out what caused the wound on Ed's neck," I mused.

Tom shrugged. "I determine if a body needs to be investigated, but I don't really have much to do with a case after that."

"You all get a lot of bodies?" Because two in a row

seemed pretty damned excessive, even from a Shifter point of view.

"No, can't say that we do. These are the first violent deaths for me since I was elected coroner two years ago. We've had a couple of unexpected or sudden deaths that I was called out for, but both of them were ruled as natural causes. I can't remember the last time this town had a homicide case, actually."

"The night of Katherine's death, did you all find something by her body?"

"Like what?"

I shook my head. "It's dumb and probably has nothing to do with anything."

"Then it won't hurt anything to tell me."

"There was a silver clip."

"A clip?"

"Like what people attach hairpieces with. An alligator clip. A small one."

His eyebrows perked up, wrinkling his forehead, and his eyes widened. "Are you sure?"

"I'm sure. It was about an inch long. Silver. Nothing attached to it."

"That's a strange thing to find next to her body."

"I thought so, but the police didn't find it. I went back to look, but it's gone now."

"Ah well, probably an animal carried it off. There are plenty at Knowles' place."

Smooshie panted hard as if stressed, reminding me her potty break was over. "We better get back now."

"Me too," he said. "I have to lock up the office."

"Lily!" I heard Parker yell.

"I'm here," I said loudly and picked up the pace.

Smooshie thought I meant to run and took off at a lope, her massive muscles yanking me forward. I lost my footing and slammed down on the sidewalk. Whoever said cats always landed on their feet, obviously never owned a cat that could walk on two legs.

"Oh man," Tom said. He reached down and grabbed me under the armpits. This close, his jacket smelled like mouthwash and antiseptic. Smooshie got the wrong impression and started growling at him, jerking my arm back as she stood over me.

Parker appeared and helped me to my feet. "Are you okay?"

There was a one-inch gash in the palm of my hand from where I'd landed on a piece of coarse gravel. "Yeah. Thanks."

Parker took Smooshie's leash, and Tom took my hand.

"It's a pretty deep cut," he said. "It needs to be stitched."

"It's not that bad," I lied. My hand throbbed as blood gushed from the wound and dripped down my fingers.

"Come to my office. I can at least get it cleaned up for you."

"You're a dentist," Parker said.

Tom looked offended. "I can handle an injured hand, Knowles."

Smooshie began tugging at her leash, barking as she scraped the pavement with her nails, trying to get back to me, but Parker kept her reined in.

"Smooshie, calm down." I grabbed a handful of snow and pressed it against the open slash to slow the blood flow. "I appreciate the offer, Tom. I can't drive like this anyhow."

"You want me to stay?" Parker asked.

"Smooshie's had enough for one day. Can you take her back to your place?"

"This won't take long," Tom added.

"All right." Parker's expression soured. "I'll take Smooshie and Elvis." He narrowed his gaze on Tom, and I saw the barest hint of a triumphant smile in the slight tug of the corner of Parker's mouth. It was the first time I realized he and Tom didn't like each other.

Nadine had said Bridgette dated Parker in high school. They were sweethearts for two years. Was Tom jealous of Parker's past with Bridgette? Or worse, was Parker jealous of Tom?

We made our way around to the front of the building. Lacy Evans stood on the sidewalk talking on her cell phone. We were far enough away that Tom wouldn't be able to hear the conversation, but I dialed up my Shifter ears and listened as we approached The Smile Factory's door.

"I said I'm fine." Her body language was rigid, her tone angry. "I had too much to drink, is all. No, I won't go to the ER. Mom, just stop. Look, I have choir tonight, and you said you'd watch Paulie. Either you will or you won't. I don't need a lecture. Just tell me if I need to come home. Fine," she said. "Thank you. I won't be out too late. Promise." She hung up and looked over at Tom and me. Her rosy cheeks paled.

"Come on," Tom said as he opened the door. He barely glanced at Lacy.

There was a giant drawing of a cartoon tooth on the right-side wall dressed as a knight, riding a drill, and holding a toothbrush as a lance. Below it was structural toys, beads on wires, puzzles, and a block station.

Thinking about Lacy, and maybe a little about myself, I said, "It's hard being a single parent."

"I wouldn't know," Tom replied. He qualified the statement by adding, "Bridgette and I want kids, we just haven't found the right time."

I could taste the bitterness of the lie. Or at least, he wasn't telling the whole truth.

"There's really no wrong or right times when it comes to children. Or so I heard."

Tom tensed his shoulders then let them droop. "We were almost parents. Once."

When I didn't respond, he continued. "Bridgette was seven months along. We lost the baby."

"Gosh, I'm so sorry. Is she doing okay?"

"I...she's had a few issues. Our obstetrician called it a post-partum depression." His face darkened with sadness as he spoke of their loss. I hated that my gift had made him tell this painful story. "That was almost two years ago."

"I bet you all will make wonderful parents when it happens."

Tom smiled. He blinked as if he'd only just realized how much he'd told me. "Bridgette did the mural on the wall. My young patients love it. They get so excited to see Sir Brushes-A-Lot."

"That's adorable."

"It was Bridgette's idea." He beamed with pride as he spoke about his wife's creativity.

"She's really talented."

"She's an artist, and that makes her a great dental technician," he said. "Bridgette can match a tooth shade on the first try. It's uncanny."

"She works with you then? You met at work?"

"I've known her my whole life."

The exam room was an eight-by-eight square with gray carpet and light-blue walls. There were two counters with drawers and cabinets on two walls. In the middle was an examination chair with a big light hanging over it. A small fountain with a drain was affixed to the right side. I'd never actually been inside a dentist's office, but it was about what I expected.

Tom turned on the water in the sink and got out some antiseptic and gauzes. Next, he donned a pair of gloves. "Let's get that washed out and see what we've got."

"I hate to keep you. I'm sure you're ready to get home."

"Bridgette has choir practice until six-thirty tonight."

"Oh yeah, they're singing for the funeral Thursday."

"The family-night visitation," Tom corrected. Gently, he washed my hand with some soap from his dispenser. It had a strong medicine smell, bitter and yucky. He patted the area with the gauze then pressed down with some clean squares. "Hold that with firm pressure. It is definitely going to need stitches."

He walked across the small room and opened a drawer. From behind, he pushed his glasses up, and I had a flash of memory from the night before. The blond man arguing with Ed. "You were at Nix's last night."

"Yes, they called me to the scene."

"You weren't there earlier?"

"Nope."

He was lying. Why?

"I could have sworn..." The look he gave me stopped me cold. "Never mind. I'd had a few drinks in me," I said as a way of apology.

Tom crossed the room back to me with a suture kit in hand. He had a small syringe with an itsy-bitsy needle filled with clear fluid. "It's lidocaine to numb the area." He squirted some of the liquid inside the wound, and the pain eased. After he had injected the area around the gouge, he poked inside and depressed the plunger until all the pain med was in my hand.

"Give it a minute and it should go completely numb."

"Dang, Tom." My palm felt thick but pain-free. "You missed your calling."

He had me lay my hand flat on a sterile sheet, then draped another one over the top like a sterile sheet sandwich, and my hand was the meat. The one on top had a hole in the middle that allowed him access to the cut.

Next, he took off his first pair of glove and put on sterile set, and laid out a small crescent moon needle with black thread attached and some sterile gauzes in the germ-free field. His conscientiousness about his work made me think he was probably a really good dentist.

He poked the inside of the wound with the needle. "Feel anything?"

"Nope. You did a good job."

He shook his head. "Honestly, I wasn't sure how much lidocaine to use for a hand. It's weird not staring down at your tonsils while working."

"They aren't that impressive," I said.

"You do have good teeth. I noticed that right away."

"Good genes."

My phone rang, and I pulled it from my pocket with my free hand. It was Parker.

"How's it going?" he asked when I answered.

"Good," I said. "Just about done here."

Tom nodded in agreement. "Two more stitches will do it."

"Did you hear that?"

"Yeah," Parker said. "As long as you're okay. Do you need a ride?"

"Nah. Martha is running smooth thanks to your dad. Quit worrying so much."

As Tom put in the last stitch, I looked around. There was a tray with a blue cloth and instruments laying out in a row. They looked like torture devices. No wonder humans hated going to the dentist.

Tom bandaged my hand and set the rolled gauze with tape. "I'll be right back," he said. "I have some antibiotic samples in my office."

"You still there?" Parker asked.

"Yep," I said. I sat on the edge of the dental chair. It was nice having someone worry about me. "I'm still here."

"I just wanted to check in."

I smiled. "You worried about me?"

"Maybe."

"That's nice." I strolled over to the counter and played with a tooth model displaying enamel erosion and advertising some product meant to fix the problem. There were white bottles with lids near the sink. One of them said Peri-lavage. The main ingredient was chlorhexidine, like the stuff Parker used on the dogs.

I opened it up and recognized the medicine and alcohol scent. The same scent I'd detected from Katherine Kapersky.

"Lily?" Parker asked at my silence.

"Oh. Oh no."

"What's wrong?" Parker asked.

"Nothing." My sense of smell wasn't proof of anything. Besides, Tom had looked genuinely ill when he'd seen Katherine's body. He couldn't fake that kind of upset, could he?

Tom came back in the room with a small box. He shook it, the packets of tablets rattling inside. "These should take care of any infection."

I took the box from Tom. "Hey, Parker. I'm just about done here."

Tom gave me an odd look as I hung up the phone. "You look like you swallowed a bug, Lily. Are you okay?"

"I'm fine," I told him. I held up my bandaged hand. "Thanks for taking care of me."

CHAPTER 20

I t was only six o'clock when I left The Smile Factory. I couldn't get over the sickening feeling I had about Tom. He had been genuinely surprised and disgusted the night I found Katherine. And I still felt like Lacy Evans was somehow involved. Maybe not directly, but the feeling that she was important, or her baby, kept nagging at me.

Tom said Bridgette was having choir practice until six-thirty, so I knew exactly where Lacy would be for a little while. Martha purred as I put her in gear. It still amazed me how well she ran.

The church parking lot had four other vehicles, two full-size trucks, a silver coup, and the rental I'd seen at the business plaza.

Apprehension tightened my skin as I parked and got out. I could hear the chorus of voices singing before I got to the door. Inside, a choir of five women and three men included Bridgette, Lacy, one of the old ladies from Buzz's diner, Opal, and the unknown deputy from the crime scene. Bridgette was standing where Katherine had been the first time I'd entered this place of worship. The dress she wore was expensive and matriarchal. Was she trying to be the new town queen?

She pointed to Lacy mid-verse, and the young mother stepped forward and sang two lines from "How Great Thou Art" with the voice of an angel. Her tone was clear and pure, a true soprano. How come she hadn't been the soloist when Katherine had been in charge?

Bridgette stopped the song with a concise swing of her hand. "That was good, Lacy, technically, but let's do it again with some feeling. Make me feel it. We want to move them to tears."

I couldn't imagine Katherine's funeral would evoke tears in anyone but her husband, Rex. However, I thought Lacy had sounded beautiful. I sat in the last pew and waited for their time to end.

Ten short minutes later, the choir was packing it in. Bridgette was talking to a short, balding man, and by her hand gestures, I could tell she was giving him notes on his singing. Lacy somberly picked up her coat and purse. She shuffled her feet down the aisle, a woman seriously disinterested in leaving. I recognized the despair and desperation. I wanted to reach out and tell her that things got better as the kid got older, that the child's independence would mean less work and struggle for her. It hadn't been the case for Danny and me, but with children, you never knew. Little Paulie could grow up to be the model of citizenship in his community. He might never give Lacy a day of trouble. Even so, she just might not have the right temperament to be a happy-go-lucky parent, no matter the circumstance. For some, it was never easy.

I felt a twinge of guilt. I wondered if it had been difficult for me because of my circumstances, an eighteen-year-old who had to switch roles from sister to mother for her seven-year-old brother, or if I just hadn't been cut out for parenting. I tried, and I had to content myself with the fact that I didn't run away from my responsibility.

Lacy stopped a few feet from the pew I sat in and rummaged in her purse before pulling out a set of keys. She saw me and gave me a startled glance.

"Hey," she said.

"Hey," I said back. "You sounded real pretty up there."

She blushed, but her smile was pleased. "Thank you. I was scared to take on a solo."

"You definitely have the voice for it."

"I used to dream about going on one of those talent shows when I was younger."

"You should have done it. I bet you would have been put through for sure."

She sat down in the row in front of me and faced back

at me. "That is so sweet of you...Lily, right? My mom told me you were her boss' cousin. I couldn't afford to go to the tryouts even if I'd been brave enough to go. Mom never made too much money." She tucked her chin. "Wow. That's probably too much information. It's just...you seem like a good listener."

"Thanks." My witchy truth mojo had a strong effect on Lacy. Good. Maybe I'd get down to the nitty-gritty of the truth. Like who the father of her child was, and why it might have gotten Katherine and Ed killed. I was like a cat with a ball of yarn on this idea. More than likely, I'd unravel the entire ball and have nothing but a mess to show for it.

"I'm sorry if I came off like a you-know-what in the office earlier. I've just been really tense the last couple of days, and I feel like everything is closing in on me."

"I get it."

"I never thanked you," she said.

"For what?"

"If you hadn't called my mom the other day, I would have been screwed." She covered her mouth. "I shouldn't talk like that in church."

"I was happy to help. I'm glad you weren't hurt."

She suddenly looked exhausted. "I'm a terrible person."

My lie detector didn't ding-ding, so she believed her confession. "I'm sorry you feel like that. Nobody tells you how hard it is to take care of another person, especially when you're on your own."

"Ain't that the truth." Her shoulders relaxed.

"Do you get any help from the father?"

Her shoulders lifted, and she held her breath for a moment. "Not much. He...I'm afraid he'll try to take Paulie from me if I push too hard. I've had social services up my butt for eight months, and the wreck this week didn't help matters. I'm afraid he'd win. He'd get my boy." She looked so young as she spoke about her worries.

"Did Katherine know who the father is?"

Her eyes were stark as she stared at me as if I'd grown a third nostril. "How'd you know?"

"I didn't. Not for sure. Your mom said she's the one that called child protective services on you."

"Not because of what she knew about Paulie's dad. She wanted me to get information..." She shook her head and smirked. "Believe it or not, she wanted my mom to give her information she could use against Buzz. She called CPS because my mom refused to help."

Freda's loyalty warmed me. She hadn't given in to Katherine's bullying. Unfortunately, Lacy had paid the cost. "The more I hear about her, the more awful she sounds."

"I think we're all being kind," Lacy said.

"When did she find out about—"

A couple of choir members passed us and said polite goodbyes to Lacy. She waved her hand at them then turned her attention back to me. "Last week. There is only one person I told. The only one who knew the truth."

"Reverend Kapersky?"

"Are you sure you're not psychic?"

"I'm sure," I said. I changed into a cougar on the full moon, and I had a little witch in me, but I was pretty sure psychic didn't play in my wheelhouse. "I saw you when you came to speak to the reverend the other day. You looked unhappy."

"I confronted him about sharing my personal business with her. Honestly, he was surprised and angry."

"Enough to kill her?"

"He's a man of God, Lily."

"Good people do bad things all the time."

Lacy frowned. "True."

Would she tell me the name of Paulie's father if I asked? Before I could gather my nerve, Lacy's eyes shifted down to my lap. "What happened to your hand?"

I held it up. "Fell down. Hard. Luckily, Tom Jones stitched it up for me."

"Oh, that's why you were going into his office."

"You saw my Tom?" Bridgette stood behind us near the door. I hadn't seen her pass by. "Lacy, don't you need to get home? We've got a big day tomorrow, and you..." she wrinkled her nose, "need a good night's sleep." Under her breath, I heard her say, "And a shower."

Lacy stood up. "I better go."

"I can walk you out."

"I'd like to talk to you for a minute, Miss Mason." She gave Lacy a pointed look that said, *Go.*

"I'll see you around," Lacy said. She put her coat on, clutching her purse to her chest as she left the building.

Bridgette plastered a perky smile on her face. "You really are a little thing. Tommy told me about you."

"Uhm..." I couldn't think of a good way to respond to her observation that wouldn't sound annoyed. "Tom told me a little about you too."

The smile faltered. "Like what?"

"He says you're a really good artist. I like what you did on the wall of his office."

She brightened again. "Oh, that." With her left hand, she coiled a ringlet of her golden hair around a finger-tip. "I like to dabble."

"You're really talented."

"Sir Brushes-A-Lot was my idea. I'm a fan of King Arthur and the Knights of the Round Table."

"I've read several books about him. It's all very romantic."

"Isn't it? Lady Guinevere had two men who were in love with her, so much that not even their friendship could stop their pursuit. And she loved them both as well."

That wasn't exactly how the story went, but I wasn't going to correct her. "Do you think it's possible to love two men equally?"

She frowned and tapped her chin. "Probably not." She looked at my hand. "What were you doing at The Smile Factory?"

"I was at the building with a friend and my dog had to go potties. I fell on the sidewalk." I didn't tell her Tom was fake smoking. Just in case she didn't know he indulged, I didn't want to be the cause of a row between them. "Tom offered to bandage it up."

"He's a good man," she said.

"How long have you two been married?"

"Five years now."

"How'd you meet?"

"I went to work for him right out of school. After a

month, he asked me out." She closed her eyes for a second. "He took me dancing in the park."

"In the park?"

"The state park, up at Ha Ha Tonka."

That sounded made up, but I didn't interrupt her to say so.

"He brought a stereo with speakers, he set up candles, and had wine, and we danced under the moonlight and stars. He treated me better than any man I'd ever been with."

"Just like a fairytale," I said.

"I hear you're staying at Parker's place."

The abrupt shift in conversation knocked me off balance. "I...uhm, yeah, I..." Used to be able to string words together to make sentences.

"Are you dating?"

This conversation had taken a strangely confrontational twist. "We... No...uh..." I'd suddenly developed the vocabulary of a toddler.

"He's damaged," she said. "You know that, right?"

"He is not," I said, finding my words again. Anger helped. "He's been through a lot, but that doesn't mean he's broken."

She gave me an *a-ha* look and pointed her left index finger at me. "So you *are* dating."

"No, we're not. I adopted a dog from him, and he's letting me stay in his garage apartment. Nothing else." Why in the world was I defending myself to this flighty woman? It was as if I'd been dosed with my own truth magic. "Why do you even care?"

She shrugged. "Because Parker broke my heart." She furrowed her brow, her eyes narrowed to slits as she stared at me. "I didn't mean that. I only meant he threw me away like trash when he joined the Army." Her eyes widened.

My anger enhanced the innate magic in me, and unfortunately for Bridgette, the truth was coming out whether she wanted it to or not.

She grabbed a set of keys from her purse. "We need to go. I promised the reverend I'd lock up after rehearsal." When she raised her arm to put on her jacket, her shirt sleeve slid up her forearm, and I saw partially healed scratches.

As we walked out. Bridgette stopped at the door to lock it. I thought about Katherine Kapersky's body. She'd smelled like Peri-lavage, and she had broken fingernails. She'd managed to put up a fight with her killer.

Impulsively, I asked, "Did you see Katherine on the day she died?"

"Yes," Bridgette said. Her face reddened. "Oh, Jesus. I didn't mean to tell you that."

"Did she come to your office?" I pressed. That afternoon, she'd complained about a hard piece of bacon. Had she really broken a tooth in the process?

"She'd cracked her crown, the stupid cow." Bridgette shook her head. "She showed up at our house at five o'clock and wanted Tom to stop everything to treat her." She clenched her fist. "At our house! It was Sunday for the love of God."

Bridgette's Mary Sunshine act had disappeared quicker than a translocating witch. "Did you kill Katherine?"

She shoved her keys down into her purse. "I don't want to talk to you anymore."

That was definitely the truth. "Did Katherine threaten you?"

"She...she was spreading lies about Tom. It was one thing for her to treat me badly, another for her to say awful things about my husband. He wouldn't cheat on me!"

Oh. Oh, hell. "He's the father of Lacy's son." That's what my intuition had been telling me. Lacy had brown hair, her kid was a blond. Like Tom. I had to be right.

"No!" She stamped her foot. "That's what Katherine said, but she's a liar! Tom wouldn't..." She shook her head in vigorous denial. "He wouldn't."

My phone rang. I took it from my pocket. It was Parker, and without thinking, I answered. "Hey."

"It's me," said Parker. "Just seeing where you're at."

"I'm…" I trailed off as I realized that Bridgette had pulled a gun from her purse and had it pointed at my head.

"Hang up," she demanded.

"I can't talk now."

"Lily, wait—"

I shoved the phone back in my pocket. "You don't want to hurt me, Bridgette."

"You'd think so," she said. "But I find I really don't mind the idea of hurting you. Not at all."

Psychopathic, but okay. "If Tom isn't Paulie's father, why would you kill Katherine?"

"I didn't say I killed her."

"Didn't you?"

"Tom got angry and got a little rough while fixing her crown. It's understandable. She just wouldn't let up. He grabbed her face a little too hard."

That explained the bruises on her face.

"She threatened to ruin him. She was going to tell the whole town about Tom and Lacy. She wanted to spread lies about my husband! He's the coroner. Everyone knows him. Us. So, I followed her when she left the office. After she left Ed's place, I followed her to her house." She looked up wistfully for a moment. "That woman was so smug. She turned her back on me, and I had a dental bib clip in my pocket." She pulled something out of her purse that looked like a nylon string with an alligator clip at each end. "It was easier than I thought it would be."

The alligator clip at the crime scene had come from the dental office. It must have caught on Katherine's coat in the struggle. "You strangled her."

She spoke as if in a dream. "Yes. Yes, I did."

"Turn yourself in, Bridgette." Tom had said she had some problems after the miscarriage. "You're suffering from post-partum depression. You might get leniency."

"All I wanted was to be a mom." I could hear a slight click as she eased the trigger of the weapon back.

"Don't," I pleaded.

Click. Boom!

The bullet tore through my shoulder and exited my back, and I staggered backward.

CHAPTER 21

I wanted to shift, to change into my cougar form and run. I wouldn't heal, but going cougar would give me the strength and speed to escape. Buzz's warning about exposing Shifters to the human world circled my brain. But as the pain went from burning to crippling, rationality was about to take a backseat to survival. Bridgette was wobbly, and I realized she'd been unprepared for the kickback of the weapon.

She took aim at me and pulled the trigger again. The bullet missed me by several feet and tore up a piece of asphalt.

Headlights lit up the parking lot, and a jolt of relief at my potential rescue gave me the energy I needed to run behind Martha. I held my left arm close to my body to keep it from moving too much. Bridgette fired two more rounds, both hitting the driver's side. Poor Martha, but when it came down to it, better her than me.

The headlights turned off as the whirring engine quieted. I needed to warn whoever it was that there was a crazy choir director on a shooting spree.

"Bridgette," a man said. "What's going on?"

It was Tom Jones. Was this a lucky break or did I just double my trouble? "She's got a gun!" I yelled from behind the front passenger wheel. I felt woozy and dizzy, as the agony of the gunshot intensified. The cougar inside me was restless, eager to claw her way out. My sense of smell, sight, and hearing all increased as pointed nails punctured my fingertips from the inside and my bones began to contract.

No, no, no. Hold it together. I couldn't allow my bleeding wound or the fear of death to trigger the shift. I couldn't expose myself.

Unless you kill them both, my inner beast said.

Luckily for the Joneses, I am not a homicidal maniac.

"Tom," Bridgette said, her voice growing small and high-pitched like a lost little girl. "I can't. I can't keep doing this."

"Put the gun down, baby. It's okay now. Just put it down."

My arms and legs felt cold as a fog rolled over my thoughts. I was losing too much blood. *Change. Change now.* Living with humans was overrated. Right? I could go back to Paradise Falls and consider this a failed adventure. How badly did I want to start a new life?

I couldn't change. Not now. Not if I ever wanted a life outside of a paranormal community.

Another shot shattered the still night. Was she still shooting at me, or had she turned on Tom?

I stuck a finger into the hole in my shoulder and screamed as agony ripped through me. I had to stop the bleeding. Had the bullet nicked my subclavian artery? It was oozing, but nothing had been spurting, and I was still awake, which meant it probably missed the big veins and arteries. Even so, the smell of my own blood made my eyes water.

Tom walked around the back side of my truck. "Let me help you," he said. I saw the gun in his left hand as he extended his right down to me.

"I can't," I told him. "If I let go I'm afraid I'll bleed to death." As the coppery scent of blood grew thicker, I worried I might pass out. "Is Bridgette okay?"

"She's fine," he assured me. "She's not going to hurt you, Lily. Not anymore."

He put the gun on the roof of Martha's cab and leaned down next to me. "I'll take care of you. I promise."

My nostrils flared at the look in his eyes. I could feel the push of his words. Not like a lie, but not the truth either.

Katherine's head, the post-mortem wound had been on the left side, and Ed, his neck wound had been on the right and in a downward slash. Only a left-handed attacker could have done either of those things.

Bridgette was right-handed.

Oh, Goddess. "Did you know Bridgette was going to kill Katherine? Did she call you that night and tell you what she'd done? Why she'd done it?"

The surprised expression on his face told me I'd hit the nail on the head. "She didn't mean to do it," he said. His hand went into his pocket, and when it came back out, Tom Jones was holding a metal dental pick, like the ones I'd seen in his office. The end curved in a half-hook, the kind of weapon that had killed Ed.

"Ed startled me. He was drunk and accused me of not living up to my responsibilities as a father."

My vision dimmed for a moment. *Dear Goddess, don't let me pass out now.* "He was her father," I said. "Ed was Lacy's father."

"Oh." He looked genuinely upset. "I can't think about that now. Bridgette is all that matters. She's in the car waiting for me."

He pulled back his arm to swing the metal pick at me— and I couldn't hold back the hollow growl that reverberated in my chest and erupted from my vocal cords.

Tom's eyes widened. "What was that?"

I didn't shift, but I let my cougar scream as I used Tom's hesitation to lunge at him. He grunted as I slammed into him. I screamed again, this time like the girl I was, because my shoulder collided with his body. I shoved him sideways into the truck and ran.

"Lily!" he shouted.

Another gun blast forced me to push past the pain and weakness. My legs were dead weights, but I knew my survival depended on my ability to stay upright.

His long strides crunched the snow as we ran through yards and between buildings. Desperation clung to me like sticky nettles when I realized he was gaining on me. I couldn't keep going. I saw a stack of fireplace wood beside a closed hardware shop. I jumped behind it, ignoring the scrapes of bark against my cheek. I grabbed my phone from my pocket, and it was lit up like a firework on the Fourth of July with the name "Parker" at the center of the screen.

I put the phone to my ear. "Parker," I said.

"Where are you?" His voice was frantic, wild. I could hear Smooshie excited noises. She was in the truck with him. "I'm trying to find you, Lily. Tell me where you are?"

Oh my Goddess, I hadn't hung up the phone. "I'm…" I double-checked the signage on the building. "I'm at Mace's Hardware behind a cord of wood."

"Stay put, Lily. I'm coming to get you."

"Call the police," I said. "Tom has a gun."

"I know." His words almost vibrated. "I heard. I heard everything."

A choking sob caught in my throat. "Hurry," I told him.

"I'm just a few minutes away. Just don't hang up, okay?"

"I won't," I whispered, but I also couldn't talk to him anymore. Not if I wanted to stay hidden.

"I know you're here, Lily Mason. Come on out. I won't hurt you. I just want to talk."

Why did bad guys always think their victims were too stupid to live? No way were we having a final chat.

There was a piece of wood about the size of Parker's bat. I couldn't grab it, not without making some kind of noise and alerting Tom to my exact location. Besides, I didn't have the strength to hold it long. I needed to reserve my energy.

"Hang on," I heard Parker say.

Off in the distance, sirens wailed. The slide of tires on pavement made my body tense. I recognized Parker's truck and Smooshie's bark. The pittie threw herself against the door, her nails scraping the window as Parker opened the driver side door. I didn't know how many bullets were left in Tom's gun, and I wanted to warn Parker, but that would give away my location.

My heart stuttered a beat when Parker walked around the front of the truck, a crowbar in hand, Tom stepped out of the shadows and pointed his 9mm at him.

Please don't get killed, I silently pleaded.

"This is priceless," Tom said. "Parker Knowles, a real hero. I'd have been happy seeing you in prison, Knowles, but dead is good too."

I couldn't let him shoot Parker. Instead, I put the target back on me and stood up. "Here! Tom. I'm right here."

He pivoted his body and the weapon at me.

"No!" Parker yelled. "The cops are coming, Tom. Can you hear them? The sirens are getting close."

"Then I best get on with it."

"It's over, Jones," Parker said. "Why are still doing this? The sheriff knows it was you."

"I promised Bridgette." He narrowed his gaze at me. "She wants you dead, Lily."

"You won't get away with this, Tom."

He blinked at me. "I don't care. I really don't."

His finger moved against the trigger, and an icy finger of terror stabbed me in the chest. I gripped the top of the wood pile. Blue and red flashing lights lit up the street a couple of blocks away.

Too late. Too late.

A howl cut through the sirens and, as if in slow motion, I watched Parker rush toward Tom.

The muzzle flashed, followed by a loud bang. Parker dove to the left and rolled up onto his feet, and kept advancing.

I became aware of a loud banging and whining from Parker's truck.

I grabbed the stick and with my good arm, I chucked it as hard as I could. The bleeding in my shoulder had slowed, but it had made me weak as heck. Which meant, I missed. However, the flying log diverted Tom's attention away from Parker for a second.

Glass shattered. Nails scraped the frozen pavement as a blur of cinnamon and white fur leaped the last ten feet to Tom Jones and knocked him to the ground.

Parker scrambled in, throwing himself on top of Tom, creating a barrier between Tom and Smooshie.

"Stop!" I shouted to my enthusiastic girl. She backed up, growling, but then ran to my side.

"Don't move, Tom, or I'll let Lily's dog tear out your throat."

Tom stopped trying to free himself. Relief flooded me as the police swarmed us. Sheriff Avery directed his deputy to arrest Tom Jones. I was vaguely aware of lying on the ground, Parker kneeling next to me and Smooshie shoving her nose under my hand.

"Hang in there, Lily. The ambulance is on its way."

"Bridgette," I mumbled. She was still out there.

"She's dead," said Avery. "Looks like a suicide."

No wonder Tom didn't care what happened to him anymore. I couldn't understand why a man who loved his wife so completely cheated on her and created a baby with someone else. I could understand Bridgette's motivations. Her husband had betrayed her in the worst way.

I was tired. Drained of both blood and energy. My eyes drooped shut.

Parker curled me to his chest, and I couldn't help but relax into his warm embrace, deeply inhaling the scents of honey and mint. "Stay with me, Lily."

"Not going anywhere," I murmured.

And then I passed out.

CHAPTER 22

The painkillers had started to wear off, and I pushed the call button for a nurse. The bullet, as I suspected had missed the major blood vessels, but they performed minor surgery to make repairs on the affected muscles and tendons. The hospital room smelled like antiseptic and body musk.

Goddess, I needed a shower.

Parker had taken Smoosh to his dad's place and returned before they finished my surgery. I was pretty out of it from the blood loss, but I remembered the panicked look in his eyes when they wheeled me in. He'd been afraid for me.

Someone knocked at the door, and I looked up in anticipation of the nurse. Instead, Buzz peeked his head inside the room. "You up for company?"

"Sure," I said. "I don't have coffee made, but the chair is comfy."

"Good enough." He brushed his hand through his hair and took a seat. "I heard about last night. You came pretty close to getting yourself killed."

"I didn't tell that woman to shoot me, nor did I ask her whack job husband to chase me down."

"No, but you did go poking your nose in affairs that weren't yours. You need to be more careful."

"I suppose you want me out of town on the next bus."

He wiggled his pursed lips than shook his head. "Nah. I think I'm okay with you sticking around. On a trial basis, of course."

"What made you change your mind?"

"You." He smiled. "You could have shifted to save yourself last night, and you didn't. If it had been me when I'd first moved into a human town, I probably would've. You showed me you're strong enough to handle it, even in the most difficult situation."

"I think you like me, Buzz Mason."

"You're family, Lily Mason. Liking you is just a bonus."

Another knock came, and Nadine walked to the bed and hugged me.

"Ow," I said. "Shoulder."

She winced. "Sorry. Jesus, what a crap-show. Tom has confessed to everything that happened. From Bridgette killing Katherine, to him putting on Parker's boots, whacking her on the head with his bat, and putting her out in the backyard. He tried to get Lacy out of the way to keep her from finding out he really was a cheater. He thought if she were dead, Bridgette would go back to her old self again."

"She'd had a miscarriage almost eighteen months earlier. It sent her into a deep depression. When Katherine told her that Tom had a baby with another woman, she snapped. He claimed Lacy seduced him during a time of grief. He hated her for it."

I sighed. "He loved Bridgette." I narrowed my gaze and shook my head. "Maybe more obsession than love."

"Creepy is what I call it," she said. "By the way, the sheriff wanted to charge you with interfering with an open and active investigation. If he could have figured out a way to take you down and still get reelected to office, he would have put handcuffs on you in the ambulance. He doesn't like being shown up by a civilian."

"I wasn't trying to embarrass him," I said. "But he was wrong about Parker."

"Speaking of Parker," Nadine segued. "He's out in the hall. You want me to go get him?"

"We'll go," Buzz said. "Give you all some time to talk."

Nadine and Buzz exited, and Parker walked in. The skitter of toenails made my heartbeat quicken.

Smooshie, wearing an emotional support dog vest, jumped up on the hospital bed. She flopped down next to me and put her head on my chest. "Hey, baby girl," I said. "Emotional support, eh?"

Parker shrugged. "It was the only way I was getting her past security."

I kissed her nose. "Thank you for coming to my rescue."

"You're welcome," Parker said.

I smirked. "I was talking to Smoosh."

He laughed. "Of course you were."

"Thanks." I blinked at him. "I don't know what would have happened if you hadn't come for me."

"I…" He rubbed his face. "You sticking around?"

"I think so." I rubbed my hand down Smooshie's warm fur. "I'll have to find a job and a place to live."

"Done and done. You can stay in the apartment as long as you want, and I just got an anonymous donation that has given me enough funds to hire two full-time employees." He met my gaze. "If you want to work for me."

"Yes," I said. My chest tightened, and tears filled my eyes. I felt stupid. And happy. Happy stupid. "I'd like that."

"Good," he said. "That's settled then. You can start as soon as you're well enough."

Another knock occurred. My hospital room was seeing more action than a werebeaver on a Saturday night. Ryan Petry, with his perfect hair and perfect face, walked in.

I gulped nervously. What the heck was the vet doing here?

"Hey, Parker," he said. "I heard Lily was here, and I wanted to check on her."

He had a handful of pink roses. Parker's face turned a bright crimson.

"Hi, Ryan." I pointed to the flowers. "Are those for me?"

He walked to the bed and handed me the arrangement. "Roses brighten a room. Or so my momma always said."

"I appreciate them. Thank you." The scent was sweet and heady. "I feel better already."

"Maybe when you get out of here, we can get that coffee."

My eyes widened at his bold offer. "We'll see."

"I'm gonna go," Parker said. His voice was strained, his tone terse. "I need to get Smooshie out of here before I get arrested."

"Thank you, Parker." When he came to get her leash, I put my hand on his. I couldn't tell him how much it meant to me that he'd brought her to the hospital. Or that he was saving me by giving me a place to live and work. Or that he'd risked his life to save me the night before. I couldn't say any of that because I was afraid if I started telling him the things I felt, I wouldn't stop at my gratitude. "Thank you."

The tightness around his eyes eased. "You're welcome. I'll see you later."

"That'd be nice." I scratched Smooshie's ears and kissed her again. "I'll see you soon, baby girl." I watched as Parker and Smooshie left the hospital room. I immediately felt bereft. For the first time in as long as I can remember, I felt like I finally had friends, family, and community. I wanted this to last. I would heed my uncle's words, but I knew it would be impossible for me not to care about these people. Heck, I already cared. I thought of Parker. A lot more than I should.

Ryan patted my arm. "You take care, Lily. I'll talk to you soon."

"Okay. Thanks for the flowers."

He offered me a smile and left.

I was feeling groggy, but just as my eyes drooped closed, a nurse appeared with a large arrangement of tiger lilies. The irony didn't escape me—my name was Lily, and I was a cat Shifter, even if I wasn't a weretiger.

"These just arrived for you," the woman said. "They're

gorgeous." She put them on a shelf and handed me the card. "Get some rest, okay?"

I nodded. When I was alone, I opened the envelope.

My heart leaped into my throat as I read the hand written note in bold block letters.

I can keep a secret. Can you?

The End... for now.

MURDER & THE MONEY PIT
BOOK 2

Chapter One

I have never been an impulsive person. I look both ways before crossing the street, I test the water with my toe before wading in, and I don't buy dilapidated, two-story rural houses.

Oh, wait. Yes, I do. The decrepit home on twelve acres of wooded land outside Moonrise, Missouri, was mine-ish. I'd just signed an "as is" rent-to-own, fifteen-year contract with Merl Peterson, a property developer, and had given him a ten grand down payment.

What have you done, Lily Mason?

"The place needs a lot of work," Merl said. His bushy eyebrows were as thick and long as the hair on his head was thin and short. "It hasn't had any work done on it in a long time. I was planning to fix it up myself for a cushy resale price, but Greer's a hard man to say no to."

"Greer's a good man," I said. "One of the best."

Greer Knowles was a mechanic in Moonrise. He owned a small garage called The Rusty Wrench. He was the very first person I met when I came to town, thanks to my green and yellow mini-truck, aka the rust bucket. I've had the truck for over twenty years now, and Martha, even with her occasional problems, was still the most reliable thing in my life. At least, she'd been the most consistent. I looked over at her. Martha's wheel well rust had gotten worse over the winter. Salted roads had a tendency to speed up oxidation. But lucky for me, Greer knew how to keep her in top running order.

Greer was also the father of my boss and friend, Parker.

My heart picked up the pace, the way it always did when I thought of Parker. I was currently living over his garage in a small studio apartment. As much as I wanted independence and a place of my own, another reason this house was so important to me was because I needed distance from Parker. It was hard working with a man I had feelings for when I knew nothing could ever come from them. Living right next to him made my heartache almost unbearable.

Merl pushed up his thick glasses and shook his head. "I have another place in town that's cheaper if this doesn't suit you."

What Merl didn't understand was that I liked the tall columns out on the porch and the ornate gables. There was something about this house, a certain charm, that I wanted to preserve.

To make mine. Besides, my pit bull Smooshie needed room to run, to be free to stretch her thick legs. Frankly, I needed the same. As a werecougar living in a human town, I didn't often have the privacy needed to shift.

Smooshie barked and yipped with manic energy. I looked over in time to see my eighty-pound brown and white pittie leaping around after an orange and black Monarch butterfly near a patch of milkweed. We'd had a warm end to winter, and spring was a couple of weeks away. Even so, seeing a butterfly this early in March was unusual. Smooshie leaped again, her whole body twisting in the air.

I smiled. I really loved that dog.

"I'll be fine, Mr. Peterson. I have plans for the place."

"I hope a bulldozer's involved," he muttered.

I didn't say "what?" because I'd heard him loud and clear. My excellent hearing was the blessing and curse of being a cougar Shifter. I could also smell the remnants of his lunch—a burger with bacon, grilled onions, and bleu cheese. Buying a house on an empty stomach was no bueno. I turned to him and said, "Thank you, Mr. Peterson. I appreciate you taking a chance on me."

"Greer says you're okay, then you're okay in my book." The older man smiled, the lines around his eyes crinkling into small canyons. "Don't mind the ghosts." He grinned now.

Parker had tried to talk me out of the place. He'd said it was haunted. His expression had been so severe that I'd tried not to laugh. Not because I didn't believe in ghosts, quite the contrary. It's just that I grew up in a town with way scarier paranormal creatures than spirits. Besides, the ghost angle had allowed me to get the place at a steal. No one wanted to live in a house where people disappeared and were never seen from again. Except me.

"If it's all right, I'd like to hang out for a while, just to get some ideas and stuff," I told Merl.

"Sure," he said. "I'll have Jock Simmons send you copies of the contract. We'll get things finalized this week."

"It's okay that I get the trailer moved over and stuff now, right?"

"Of course. The place is yours. Just need to dot the i's and cross the t's, but as far as I'm concerned, you are home."

I smiled. "Sounds good." When Merl left, I pulled out my phone and made a call. "Haze. I got the house," I said when my BFF answered.

"Oh. Em. Gee!" She materialized and hugged me hard. "That's amazing."

Smooshie's barking grew even more excited, almost verging on a frantic hysteria as she danced around Hazel, going up on two feet, but not quite jumping on her.

"Will you muzzle your beast?" a squeaky voice demanded. A red squirrel climbed Haze to get away from my pittie.

"She's just saying hello, Tiz." I scratched Smooshie behind the ear, and she leaned her thick body into me, her tail whacking the back of my thighs as she panted her pleasure.

Hazel Kinsey is a witch, and Tizzy, a squirrel, is her familiar. They were both my best and only friends when I was growing up. Being short and skinny in a Shifter community was the same as being weak and useless. I'd never wanted to stay in Paradise Falls, but the death of my parents had made that choice for me. I'd had to drop out of high school to support my little brother, and I stayed until he died. It still hurt to think of Danny. There was nothing left for me there once he was gone.

"Is this it?" Tizzy asked. She made a chittering sound of disgust. "What a dump."

"Tiz!" Haze crossed her arms. "It just needs a little TLC. And maybe a little…" She wiggled her fingers.

"No magic," I said.

"Not even a little?"

"She's probably worried you'll blow her house down." Tizzy jumped to my shoulder. "Not that it would take much. Did you find this place in Deader Homes and Gardens?"

"Ha ha. Very funny."

"I thought so." Tizzy pulled an almond from somewhere on her furry person—I didn't want to know from where—and began to chew. "I like all the trees. And oh, look! Squirrels." Two gray squirrels ran up a mature maple. I rolled my eyes.

Haze, who was taller than me by six inches, put her arm around my shoulders. "You'll make it a real home, Lily. I have every faith."

"Thanks for lending me the down payment."

She smiled. "I know you're good for it." She gave me a squeeze.

"I'm kind of scared, Haze."

My BFF put her hands on my shoulders and stared down at me. "Why?"

"I'm not sure I can make it out here." By "out here" I meant in an entirely human town. Well, mostly. I'd never had to hide before, and I wasn't sure I could keep it up. "Aside from the fact that I'm a fish out of water—"

"More like a cat out of the litter box," Tizzy snarked.

I ignored her. "I didn't even finish high school. I don't make enough working at the shelter to afford a mortgage and food." Shifters burned through calories like fire burned through a month-old Christmas tree. And I needed a lot of protein in my diet, too. "Have you checked out the price of beef lately? It's ridiculous. I could spend a paycheck on red meat alone."

"Have you thought about getting your GED, maybe taking some classes at the local college?"

"I don't know."

"You're the smartest person I know, Lily Mason. It would be a shame to let all those brains go to waste."

Hazel believed every word she said. I could smell the truth on her. It was a gift passed down from my great-great-grandmother on my mother's side, who happened to be a witch, amazingly enough. I only found out in October that I wasn't pure Shifter, and some dangerous magic back home had triggered my ability as a truth-sayer. Most people wanted to be truthful, anyhow, and my power allowed them to open up to me. It didn't always work. If someone wanted to hide a secret bad enough, they could resist the compulsion to come clean.

I nodded to my friend. "I won't give up."

"Good, because you've been happy here, Lils. More happy

than I'd ever seen you before." She squeezed my shoulders. "Humans are good for you."

"Yeah, yeah." I could hear the roar of a dually truck engine less than a mile away. "My boss is coming. You better get out of here."

"The boss?" She made *the* sound like *thee*. "The one who basically rescued you and swept you off your feet?"

"Stop," I said. "Seriously. You need to go."

Haze's phone played "Bear Necessities" from *The Jungle Book*. "Shoot, that's Ford." She looked at the screen. "It's a 9-1-1. There's been trouble since Halloween between the Shifters and the witches, and with spring right around the corner, it's not getting any better." She kissed my cheek. "Call me if you need me."

"I'll be fine," I told her and gave her a quick hug.

"Bye, Lils!" Tizzy said as she circled her witch's waist and climbed up her back. "Next time leave your beast at home."

I knelt next to Smooshie, who happily wagged. "She is home."

Tizzy stuck her tiny tongue out at me. Haze gave me a wistful smile. "Tell lover boy I said hello."

"He's not—" They disappeared before I could finish my protest. Parker's big black truck was throwing dust up as it came down the gravel drive.

The truck ground to a halt about thirty feet away. Parker rubbed his hand over his dark hair before he opened the driver-side door and stepped out. He was average height, about five feet eleven inches, which was still eight inches taller than me. I'd always been a bit of a runt. He had a broad chest, muscular arms, and crystal-blue eyes that nearly undid me every time he looked my way.

His dog Elvis—half pit bull, half horse—jumped out of the truck after him. The large, silvery-blue beauty hugged his body against his master's legs. As a PTSD dog, Elvis had been trained to pick up on Parker's body language and put himself between Parker and stressors. Turns out I was one of those stressors. I didn't want to make Parker's life difficult. Just the opposite. It was the reason I needed my own place.

"Whatcha doing out here?" I asked, shielding my eyes from the sun as he approached. An easy breeze carried his scent to me, and I fought the urge to run into his arms. We were friends. Nothing more. No matter what my Shifter libido wanted.

"I have to run into Cape Girardeau for some supplies, and dad asked me to bring you out his toolbox, shovel, and plaster scraper." He reached into the bed of the truck and lifted out a red bifold-topped metal box.

"It's so I can bury the bodies."

Parker froze for a moment. A crooked smile played on his lips. "You need help? I got a hacksaw back home."

I laughed. "These will do." I took the shovel and scraper from him. I followed him to the porch where he set the toolbox down.

"There you go," Parker said. He rubbed his hands on his jeans and put them in the pockets of his windbreaker.

"Tell Greer I owe him some pie." It was a joke between us. Parker's dad and I shared a love of food in a pastry.

"I'll let him know." His low voice always made my stomach jittery.

Smooshie and Elvis sniffed each other, with Smooshie getting her full nose right up his butt. I didn't want to begrudge her the formal dog greeting of an old friend, but automatically, I said, "Stop that."

Smooshie cocked her head at me, gave Elvis one more nose goose then moved away. Thank heavens Elvis tolerated Smooshie. He outweighed her by at least thirty pounds.

"You sure you want to live out here?" Parker asked. "It's going to take a lot of work to get this place livable."

"Buzz is moving in with Nadine. He's going to let me put his trailer out here to live in until I can get it all fixed up."

Buzz was actually my uncle and was a good forty years older than me, but since we were both Shifters, we could pass for nearly the same age. Nadine was one of the few friends I'd made since I moved to Moonrise. She was a deputy sheriff for the county, and she was very much in love with my uncle. Unfortunately, she could never be Buzz's mate. Oh, he loved Nadine. He probably loved her as much as she loved him, but Buzz was a werecougar.

A Shifter. The only other nonhuman in town besides me.

Shifters only mated with other Shifters, with only a few exceptions, and all of those exceptions were paranormal mates. There was a distinct aroma that developed between mates, and when a Shifter caught the scent, it was for life. That couldn't happen in a Shifter-human relationship. It was genetically impossible. But since Buzz hadn't ever found his true mate, he and Nadine could be happy for many years together. Sadly, it would eventually end. And that was another reason to not get involved with sexy humans like Parker Knowles.

I felt an aching pain in my heart. My kind lived a very long time. Hundreds of years sometimes. I'm not sure anyone is built to watch the people they love grow old and die. I know I'm not.

"So Buzz is taking the big step, huh?" Parker smiled, his blue eyes lighting up with mischief. "He seems more like the rambling kind than the settling-down kind."

"Nadine has a way of getting what she wants." She reminded me a lot of Hazel. Nadine was very straightforward, a lot of "what you see is what you get." I admired her bluntness and her honesty.

I smiled at Parker; a melancholy feeling that I'd grown accustomed to experiencing washed over me. I knelt down, feeling the sudden need to hold on to something, in this case, my pittie. Smooshie put her wet nose to my ear and licked my cheek. I patted her.

"Theresa holding down the fort today?" I asked. She was Parker's other paid employee. He could only afford to have us both on part time thanks to an anonymous donation that rolled in every month on the fifth. Theresa Simmons, who had started as a volunteer, had worked at the Pit Bull Rescue Center for over two years. Parker also had several volunteers who spent time socializing the rescue dogs to get them ready for rehousing.

"Keith, Jerry, and Emily are in today, so she has plenty of help."

"Good, I hated leaving you short on a Saturday. I know that's when you run your errands, but it was the only time Mr. Peterson had open to meet with me."

"Life happens." He glanced over at me, his blue eyes locking on my gaze. "They don't get much better than Merl Peterson. He gave me my first job, did you know that?"

"No, you never told me."

"Yeah, he likes to hire local teenagers for odd jobs. He'd hire me occasionally for things like deck building and roofing. Summer work. It was long hours but a decent paycheck."

"My first job I clerked at a convenience store. I worked nights and some weekends." I'd had to quit school to work full-time, and the Valhalla Gas & Go was the only place that would hire an eighteen-year-old dropout.

"I'm glad you're putting down roots here." He looked around, his upper lip curled a little in disgust. "Even if it's this place."

"The house has good bones," I told him.

"That's not a house."

"It has doors and windows and rooms and—"

"Ghosts."

"Parker."

"Facts are facts, Lily." He walked up the front steps as if drawn, his voice like that of a tour guide. "Randall Dilley, who built the place back in 1908, hung himself in the living room. Another owner, Lincoln Edwards, was killed in a combine accident in the 1940s, a whole family disappeared from here in the eighties, and there hasn't been someone living there since Old Man Mills died in the upstairs bedroom two years ago."

"Let me guess." I mockingly gasped. "He was murdered."

"Nah. Natural causes." Parker paused. "Or so they say…" He let it hang there as if to imply there were more sinister reasons behind the old man's death. What he didn't realize is, because of my witch ancestor's gift, I could smell bull-poop from a mile away.

Anyway. I knew a little about John "Old Man" Mills. The property had been held in escrow as the court tried to find a blood relative somewhere to inherit. No one came forward, so the property was sold to Merl—who'd sold it to me.

"You want to go on the supply run with me?" Parker asked.

"No thanks." I smiled. "Another time. I want to get in and measure the rooms. I need to figure out where I want to start with this place. Besides, Buzz is bringing out the trailer today."

"That's fast." His lips thinned. "Well, thought I'd ask."

"And I appreciate it." To lighten the mood, I asked, "Do you think the ghosts took him out?"

"Who?"

"Old Man Mills, of course."

"I think he's one of the ghosts now." He moved in close, his tone ominous. "Some say when the moon is full, and the wind is right, you can smell his farts on the breeze."

I giggled. "That's terrible."

I will not flirt with Parker. I will not flirt with Parker. It had become my mantra. A mantra that failed fifty percent of the time.

I knew Parker liked me. A lot. I could scent his attraction. For whatever reason, his desire for me smelled like honey and mint. Crisp, refreshing, and exciting. But he deserved to be with a woman he could grow old with, and I had a terrible feeling that if I allowed myself to love Parker Knowles, I wouldn't be able to give him up when the time came for me to leave Moonrise. I could only stay for so long before people would start asking questions about why I didn't age, and the first rule of integrating with humans was to never let them know you were different. Not unless you wanted to be hunted down like an animal.

Humans had two impulses when it came to things they didn't understand. Kill it or dissect it. I didn't want either of those things happening to me.

One-Click "Murder & The Money Pit" To Read More!

PARANORMAL MYSTERIES & ROMANCES

BY RENEE GEORGE

Witchin' Impossible Cozy Mysteries

www.witchinimpossible.com

Witchin' Impossible (Book 1)

Rogue Coven (Book 2)

Familiar Protocol (Booke 3)

Mr & Mrs. Shift (Book 4)

Barkside of the Moon Mysteries

www.barksideofthemoonmysteries.com

Pit Perfect Murder (Book 1)

Murder & The Money Pit (Book 2)

The Pit List Murders (Book 3)

Peculiar Mysteries

www.peculiarmysteries.com

You've Got Tail (Book 1) FREE Download

My Furry Valentine (Book 2)

Thank You For Not Shifting (Book 3)

My Hairy Halloween (Book 4)

In the Midnight Howl (Book 5)

My Peculiar Road Trip (Magic & Mayhem) (Book 6)

Furred Lines (Book7)

My Wolfy Wedding (Book 8)

Who Let The Wolves Out? (Book 9)

Madder Than Hell

www.madder-than-hell.com

Gone With The Minion (Book 1)

Devil On A Hot Tin Roof (Book 2)

A Street Car Named Demonic (Book 3)

Hex Drive

https://www.renee-george.com/hex-drive-series

Hex Me, Baby, One More Time (Book 1)

ABOUT THE AUTHOR

I am a USA Today Bestselling author who writes paranormal mysteries and romances because I love all things whodunit, Otherworldly, and weird. Also, I wish my pittie, the adorable Kona Princess Warrior, and my beagle, Josie the Incontinent Princess, could talk. Or at least be more like Scooby-Doo and help me unmask villains at the haunted house up the street.

When I'm not writing about mystery-solving werecougars or the adventures of a hapless psychic living among shapeshifters, I am preyed upon by stray kittens who end up living in my house because I can't say no to those sweet, furry faces. (Someone stop telling them where I live!)

I live in Mid-Missouri with my family and I spend my non-writing time doing really cool stuff...like watching TV and cleaning up dog poop.

Follow Me On Bookbub!